
SEDUCED BY AN ALIEN WARLORD

AVA ROSS

Foreword

A note to the reader.

If you found this book outside of Amazon,
it's likely a stolen/pirated copy.
Authors make nothing when books are pirated.
If authors are not paid for their work,
they can't afford to keep writing.

*For my mom who
always believed I could do this.*

*For my hubs & kids, who puts up with
"hey, let's eat this" ten minutes
before dinnertime.*

*Thanks to my new air fryer.
(see above)*

*And special thanks to some awesome
readers who jump in and help
me make my books better.
Alex, Deonne, Jenny, Joy,
Kristin, Laura, Meg, & Stephanie.*

Seduced by an Alien
Warlord

**He's a proud alien warlord.
She's a single mom hoping to find love again.
When their worlds collide, sparks fly.**

Bruge: I'm a serious warlord, not a youngling warrior in need of a mate. Ensuring the duskhorde don't kill us and that the clan gathering runs smoothly is enough to keep me busy. Court an Earthling female? Perhaps later. But when I meet Alexa, my second heart starts beating, proving she's my maelstrom mate. Now I want her, and the best way to claim her is with an ancient Ferlaern tradition: abduction and seduction. If only my entire village would stop trying to help make it happen.

Alexa: I've crushed on Bruge for a while. He's grumpy, gruff, and he has interesting social skills. What's not to like? A widow raising three-year-old twin boys, I still have room in my life for romance. But whenever Bruge and I get close, we either wind up in trouble or we're interrupted. Even better? His warriors follow us around snickering. Our relationship is going nowhere fast, but I'm not giving up, because there's more than one way to seduce an alien warlord.

Seduced by an Alien Warlord is Book 3 in the Fated Mates of the Ferlaern Warriors Series. This standalone, full-length romance has on-the-page heat, aliens who look and act alien, a guaranteed happily ever after, no cheating, and no cliffhanger. Look for the complete series on Amazon.

Books by AVA

MAIL-ORDER BRIDES OF CRAKAIR

Vork

Bryk

Jorg

Kral

Wulf

Lyel

Axil, Gaje

(companion novellas in one book)

BRIDES OF DRIEGON

Malac

Drace

Rashe

Teran

Kruze, Allor

(companion novellas in one book)

IN LOVE WITH AN ALIEN ANTHOLOGY

Neere

a Brides of Driegon short story

ALIEN EMBRACE ANTHOLOGY

Skoar

a Brides of Driegon novella

FATED MATES OF THE FERLAERN WARRIORS

Enticed by an Alien Warlord

Tamed by an Alien Warlord

Seduced by an Alien Warlord

Tempted by an Alien Warlord

You can find all my books on Amazon.

Before
ALEXA

Two years ago, a disease swept across Earth, killing most of the adult men, including my husband. We mourned. I wanted to rip out my hair and cry all day long, but my twin sons were thankfully spared. They kept me busy and gave me a reason to go on. I could do it for them, if not for myself.

The loss of our men not only ripped them from our arms, but we also lost our chance of a future. It sounds clinical, but how could we reproduce with so few men? We resigned ourselves to a drastic population reduction over the next hundred years due to the lack of men.

Then a ping reached us. Aliens existed and they were eager to meet Earthlings. After watching alien invasion movies, we worried they'd take over our world, but they truly came in peace.

Our dignitaries met with theirs, and treaties were formed. They sent advanced technology that pulled us into the next century.

They announced they'd lost their women to the disease and after we grew comfortable with them, they suggested something unbelievable. Why not arrange matches between our two species? Geneticists jumped in and analyzed us, discovering we were compatible. Those accepted into the new matchmaking program were given translators to help smooth the transition, though they were faulty.

In our first adventure into space, a few groups of women traveled as mail-order brides for seven-foot-tall, green scaled aliens on a planet called Crakair. When these matches were wildly successful, new arrangements were made with a species called Driegons living deep below Crakair's surface.

Now another planet has sent us a message.

We are the Ferlaern, a noble species. Hunters, warriors, and riders of mighty, winged trundier. We are fearless and passionate.

Here is our offer: Settle on Ferlaern, and we will court you. Seduce you. Win you. When matches are made, we will provide for you and any young you might gift us.

As a widow with two rambunctious three-year-old boys, I wasn't sure I wanted to become a "mate," as they called their wives. I still mourned my husband.

But... I was lonely and my boys needed a father figure in their lives.

So, I sucked in a deep breath and applied for the program, convincing myself I'd never be accepted.

I was.

Once I arrived on Ferlaern, I met Bruge. Despite his gruff manner, he sparked a part of my heart I thought had died. Then he took off and I didn't see him again for months.

Now the four migratory Ferlaern clans are gathering in the lowlands to spend the winter months together. I imagine I'll run into Bruge.

And this is my story...

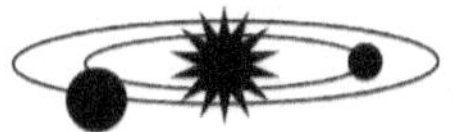

Bruge

Our Ferlaern Clans would gather in the lowlands over the next few sunslices, and while I looked forward to visiting with everyone, there was one Earthling female I was eager to see most of all.

Alexa.

I finished the final touches on the domit I'd present to her when she arrived. Had I done too much? She was worthy of my best efforts, but Earthlings were complicated.

Too damn confusing.

It was hard to know what might offend her. From the short time I interacted with her, I could tell she was assertive and independent. She wouldn't enjoy a heavy hand.

As a female worthy of a clan warlord, perhaps she wished to finish the construction of her own domit? Many Ferlaern females do.

Glancing around the interior one last time, I contemplated what else I could do to make her feel welcome. I heard Earthling females enjoyed flowers, but few grew on this region of the plain. I doubted she'd enjoy a bouquet of drended stems as they were apt to bite if someone came close. And the pularn blossoms would take up half a room. Perhaps I could squeeze a few truedrops into the small vegetable garden behind the domit.

This unit was a bit larger than most, but she had two younglings. Her sons would need their own space. The central portion contained a living area, and I crafted two attached bedrooms, one for her and the other for her younglings.

Wait. What if I—

The flap of winged trundiers made my two hearts skip several beats. Turning, I pushed aside the door flap and stepped outside, my gaze seeking the sky. Was Alexa arriving?

From the munette I met her, she called to me. I ached to run my fingers through her hair the color of ripened worthisk grains. To touch her curvy form. When she watched me with her dark blue eyes stormier than the river cutting through the plain behind our village, my second heart seized.

She was my fated maelstrom mate. Finding the symbol on my shoulder only confirmed what I already knew. My second heart came to life the munette I saw her.

Now to convince her she was mine.

"They are here," my mother said, walking up beside me. A sneer filled her bronze face, creasing her segmented skin. A breeze caught her lavender hair, making the black strands glisten. "Earthings." She spat. "You heard what happened with Durran, did you not?"

"Yes," I said, striving for patience. "He told me himself." And she'd told me at least five times.

"He left the Suthen Clan."

"His uncle passed on his powldron." I ran my fingers

across my own powldron I'd bonded with eight cycles ago, before my father died.

"He left because of *her*."

"Not completely. His father…" I growled, not wishing to go through this again. My mother did not like the Earthlings, and nothing would change that.

"I, for one, will not be here to greet them," she said with a huff. She spun on her heel and stalked toward the opposite side of the village.

I pushed my irritation with her aside. Now was for greeting Alexa.

A trundier screeched overhead as a large flight of them circled. Recognizing the beasts from the Osten Clan, my excitement waned. The mighty winged creatures dropped to the ground beyond the fence.

My friend, Zetar, slid off his beast and gave it a long pat before striding over to where I remained outside Alexa's domit. I'd crafted it from the most attractive wuldra husks, suspecting a female's heart might take joy in living within something pretty. The plant's broad leaves were easily woven into a tight mesh, making them impervious to water and…

And they…*spanked*. No, that was not the correct word. They *sparkled*.

Warriors from Zetar's Clan strode past us, heading toward the wuldra trees growing along the riverbank. They'd harvest leaves to encase their own, skeletal domits. Soon, our village would come alive again.

Each cycle, our clans spent the hot summer months in domits hidden deep within the mountain valleys. There, we bonded with trundier hatchlings and began their training. During the relatively cooler winter months, we migrated to the lowlands. Here, we hunted the warslettes, cleaning and drying their meat to enjoy while living in the mountains. Hunting was scarce in the hills; many of the creatures are consumed by the ferocious liscards.

"You won't believe what I saw not far from here," Zetar said grimly. His feet scuffed the dry soil and the wind swept it up and carried it across the endless plain. He turned his squinted gaze to the deep golden, wavering grasses. "A large tribe of duskhorde are crossing the northern plain, heading toward our mountain valleys."

I lifted a hand toward my second-in-command, Frelz, and he strode over, his heavy gaze passing between us.

"You should hear this," I said, nudging my head to Zetar, who repeated what he saw.

"Do you think they hope to take over our summer domits in the mountains?" Frelz asked. "It makes no sense."

"Of what use are our domits without trundiers?" Zetar wisely asked. "This is why we choose to live there."

"And the trundiers travel with us," I said. Only a few unbonded beasts remained in the mountains. They would resist any dusklen who tried to take up residence in the trees.

I didn't like this, though I couldn't point to what made unease grind through me like a jagged blade. Skirmishes with the duskhorde were relatively uncommon, so them passing across the plain even in a large group could be ignored unless they approached our winter village. But heading into the mountains? They rarely traveled there other than in small packs to raid eggs and hatchlings, and the remaining mature adult trundiers could protect themselves from the horde.

"We could speculate for sunslices and not understand why they do anything," I finally said.

Frelz raked his fingers through his black hair shot through with only a few strands of purple. I'd inherited more of a lavender coloring from my mother and had only a few bands of black. My height and deeper bronze skin came from my father. "They drove a sizeable herd of warslette."

Interesting. The herds were plentiful in the lowlands. I wasn't necessarily worried about the duskhorde claiming what they needed. We all had to eat, and I'd rather the duskhorde consume warslette than us.

"Perhaps they plan to take the narrow passage through the far edge of the mountains," I said. "I heard other dusklen tribes live in the valleys beyond." Concern filled me, keeping me unsettled. I nodded to Frelz who likely knew what I was thinking already. "Wing after them. Follow them to see what they do, but don't let them know you're watching. Once you've determined their plan, report back. By then, the rest of the clans will have arrived, and we can discuss how best to handle this."

"Very well." Frelz pressed his fist against his chest. He spun and strode toward the trundier flock. His mount soon winged into the sky, and I watched until they merged with the horizon.

"The Earthling females will be here soon," Zetar said, rocking on his heels. He flashed his tusks in irritation.

"You as well?" I asked.

"Not all of them." Zetar scowled. "Just one."

"Which one in particular?"

Zetar shook his head. "It does not matter."

Yet here he was, letting one irritate him. Which female had caught his eye?

"Alexa will be with them," I said. Even speaking her name made my pulse surge.

Zetar had seen my matebond symbol. He knew my thoughts about this particular female. So did Durran. I told him of my interest in Alexa when I visited his clan many sunslices ago. If only I'd seen her then, but when I looked for her, I couldn't find her. Someone said she was in the community domit, singing, and as much as I ached to hear her lilting voice in song, the demands of my clan needed to come first.

They should all the time. Why couldn't I stop thinking about her, doing things for her? My father had been the unofficial lead warlord when the clans gathered on the plain. I had stepped into this role when his powldron fused to my shoulder. There would not be time this cycle to court a female.

"Will you claim Alexa?" Zetar asked.

I snorted. "The true question is, will she be willing to be claimed?"

"She has younglings. They keep her busy." He scratched the back of his neck. "They will take up much of her time."

"She cannot be too busy for mating, I don't believe. Her younglings are a gift."

Zetar cocked his head. "Have you interacted with them? I have, and they are more than one handful. At least three or four."

"I welcome the task of taming them."

"As well as Alexa," Zetar said with a flash of his tusks. "How do you plan to win her? Will you use the standard courtship rituals or experiment with those of the Earthlings?" He scowled again. "Their expectations are too steep."

Ah, so that's how this was. Had he tried to court one of the Earthlings already?

"I thought I might try one of our ancient traditions," I said.

"Such as?"

My lips curved up. "Abduction and seduction."

Alexa

As I rode with an older Ferlaern warrior on his trundier, I was a jumble of nerves.

One of my mischievous sons winged with me, and he kept trying to stand on the beast until I spoke sharply to him. Then he sulked before dropping to sleep. Yet his antics weren't enough to hold my complete attention.

I couldn't shake the feeling someone was watching me. Spinning around, I scanned the other trundiers flying nearby, each mounted with one or two Ferlaern.

None stared my way. A grunt slipped out of me. I needed to shrug off the uneasy feeling.

It was silly, actually. Of course the Ferlaern watched us. We were new here. Only a few of us were still available for mating matches. And we were women, a hot commodity after they lost most of their females to the disease.

Another reason I was on edge was because of Bruge, the warlord of the Osten Clan. I only met him briefly last spring when he and the other Ferlaern arrived to help build our settlement. After the duskhorde attacked, and our construction materials burned, we moved to the mountain valley instead.

Now we migrated to the lowlands, where the four Ferlaern Clans spent their winter months—moons, that is. I'd finally see Bruge again.

Did he remember me?

My friend, Josie, flew in closer to the trundier I rode on. She waved and smiled, and with the flap of the wings, I could barely hear her. But we'd gotten good at yelling and flying the beasts close together without the beasts hitting wings.

"Frurok here says we'll be there soon," she said, tilting her head to the warrior she rode with. Her brown skin gleamed in the sunlight. "Nothing against riding on a beastie for transportation, but I can't wait to put my feet on solid ground." Leaning forward, she looked down and shuddered. Most of us didn't mind the height, but let me tell you, zipping through the air hundreds of feet above the ground on a creature that looked like a giant hornet was enough to shake the spirit of even the stiffest of our group.

Josie kept a tight arm around my other son, Will's waist while I held onto his three-year-old twin brother, Ben. Thankfully, other than a few attempts to "fly," the boys slept for most of the four-day journey. I had to admit, if only to myself, my sons were a handful. Of course, now that they were taking power naps, they'd be their rambunctious selves the moment we landed.

Despite my occasional groan in response to their antics, I wouldn't have them behave in any other way. They were growing up too fast. Where had the tiny babies I used to cradle on my lap gone?

"Ugh, are we gonna be there soon?" Another, smaller trundier soared up to float level with Josie's, carrying her thirteen-year-old daughter, Savvy. "Are we there yet? Are we there yet?" Savvy rolled her brown eyes to show she was joking. She shoved a band of her dark, tightly curled hair back behind her ear, looking so much like her mom, I grinned.

She was the only Earthling not riding with someone else. For some reason, one of the unbonded youngling trundier females took a liking to her. The creature followed her overhead when she walked along the canopy paths. And it would land in an empty nest and stare out at Savvy whenever she played with the hatchlings. Savvy started working with the trundier under the direction of our trainer, and the two were now nearly inseparable. When we were preparing to leave, the youngling pup flew in and landed beside Savvy, nudging her side with her snout, telling Savvy she wanted to travel with us. The creature needed more training, so for now, she remained close to Josie's mount.

"It will not be long now," the warrior guiding Josie's mount told Savvy. "Do not be impatient, youngling."

Savvy huffed, and I knew she hated being called a child, but she wasn't fully grown yet. She still maintained that leggy, pre-teen shape, much to her disgust.

We flew above the last bit of scruffy forest in the lower area surrounding the mountain peaks and out over an enormous plain made up of pale golden grass. A few trees peppered the landscape, but this section of Ferlaern was a stark contrast to the mountain canopy I'd lived in since we arrived on this planet.

Ahead, I spied hundreds of low buildings crafted from something only slightly darker than the plain. A few fenced-in areas spread into the distance to the right of the buildings, and a wide river flowed in a snaky fashion behind, winking in the sunlight.

Trundiers resting on the ground in one of the pens

fretted, spying us coming near. They rose as we approached, screeching cries of welcome.

We circled overhead and then swooped down to land near the others. Dull thuds of clawed feet impacting with the ground rang out, and dust swirled around us before it dissipated in the wind.

"Thank you for the ride," I told the warrior.

He grunted, which was pretty much the extent of his conversation over the past four days. His arm had remained loosely around my waist, his touch purely paternal, which beat the groping I got from the first guy I rode with after we left the mountains. Just because I sat in front of someone, it didn't mean I was open to him pinching my boobs.

"We're here, sweets," I told Ben, stroking the damp hair off his sweaty brow.

He moaned and whimpered, shifting on my lap. "Sleepy."

"I bet you are, but we've arrived in the lowlands where we'll spend the winter moons. It's time to wake up."

His eyes opened, and he blinked slowly as he took in the inky brown trundiers crouched around us. When I first saw them, I cringed. My friend, Piper, who was now mated with our clan warlord, pegged the beasts as giant hornets, and I had to agree with her assessment.

To think I'd been afraid to ride them at first. But after traveling for days, you almost got used to it.

The warrior slid off the beast and held his hands up to take Ben from me.

I handed off my son and accepted the male's help down. My feet landed on the ground, and I wavered, grabbing onto the trundier's scaled hide.

The warrior strode to the beast's head and gave it a pat. He located a bucket and filled it from a stone trough then brought it over for the creature to drink. His gaze fell on me, and he grunted again.

In other words, get to it, Alexa. Leave the beastie alone.

With Ben hauling on my arm, I half-ran around the creature to Josie's trundier to collect my other son.

She stood holding onto Will's arm while he leaped with excitement.

"We here. We here!" he said, staring around. He must've spied the river. "We goin' swimmin'?"

"Not so fast, short stop," Josie said, fisting the back of his shirt to hold him in place.

"I'll take him, and thanks," I said.

That uneasy feeling crept over me again, and I shivered despite the warm day.

A glance over my shoulder showed nothing but the warrior I rode with unloading our belongings from the back of his mount. Other Ferlaern strode away from the pen, toward the half-constructed village. A few nearby took care of their mounts and belongings. My gaze swept the plain nearby, but I spied nothing but wavering grasses. No, maybe not grass. Some sort of grain.

"I'll leave your belongings here?" the warrior I rode with asked, waving to our stuff. We hadn't brought much, mostly clothing, as we were told everything we needed would be provided here.

"Thank you." After I got the boys settled in our new home, I'd come back for our bags.

My gaze was caught by... I squinted toward the long rows of buildings, but whatever I saw didn't reveal itself. I shrugged. It had to be nothing.

As Josie, Savvy, and me and the boys left the trundiers and strolled toward the long rows of buildings constructed from what looked like long, thick, woven corn husks, I wondered where we'd sleep tonight. I was told the inner structures remained for many years, but the outer siding had to be replaced each cycle. I might have a lot of work to do before dark.

Because I couldn't help myself, I watched for Bruge as we passed one burly group of Ferlaern warriors after another.

They were universally bronze, and their segmented skin shifted as they moved. Majestic horns jutted off their heads, and their long tails coiled up behind them, avoiding the dust.

Like a Navy Seal team with various weapons poking out of the straps crisscrossing their chests, they looked ready to defeat an entire tribe of duskhorde.

I shivered from the memory of the hairy aliens attacking us not long after we arrived on this planet.

"Looking for anyone in particular?" Rayne asked as she sidled in close to me.

"Oh, no one." I grinned. She knew me too well.

Her daughter, Missy, walked with her. Durran, Rayne's new maelstrom mate, wasn't with them, but I imagined he'd—

He playfully growled as he rushed up behind her to sweep her off her feet.

Rayne laughed and, looping her arms around his shoulders, kissed his neck.

I looked away, overcome with envy. Durran and Rayne were essentially newlyweds, though they weren't marrying for another month or so. I was helping her make her dress. They connected when we lived in the mountain valley, falling for each other while investigating who was trying to poison the mighty trees. We lived in big blossoms suspended from the trees, high in the treetops. Once they figured out what was killing the trees and took care of the bad guy doing the deed, Elder Narcial came up with a concoction to cure the trees. When we left the valley, they were thriving again.

Rayne nuzzled Durran, her fingers trailing through his long black hair shot through with purple.

What would it be like to have someone love me as much as Durran did Rayne? My husband had at one time, but he'd never been this spontaneous, especially after everything we went through to have the boys.

"Me, me!" Missy cried, dancing around him, and calling my attention back to her. "I wanna be carried, too!" She laughed and tugged on the weapon holster around his waist until he lifted her with his other arm and dropped her on his shoulder. She clung to his horns and gazed around. "Wow. I can see far!"

He stopped on the wide path and kissed Rayne.

Josie rolled her brown eyes, and she and I kept walking. Durran and Rayne would catch up eventually, or we'd see them later.

They were lost in each other, and it made my heart burn. Maybe someday…

It was silly to long for someone I'd only spoken with only a few times. Our fingers brushed together once, and the spark that simple touch lit inside me wouldn't take much fanning to turn it into a roaring blaze.

Did he even remember me?

I came to this planet to meet someone for a lasting relationship. When I boarded the ship from Earth, I made myself step out of the shell I fell into after my husband died. I loved him, and a part of me went with him to the grave. I'd lived for my boys for the first year, then started to live for myself after that. While I missed him, it would be wrong to spend my life mourning. Liam wouldn't want that; he said so as he lay dying. *Go on, Alexa. Find happiness. Think of me and smile, but don't spend your life feeling sad.*

It hadn't been easy but here I was, contemplating a relationship with a male from an alien species.

But I'd never met someone who stirred me like Bruge did.

"I'm stupid to be thinking about him," I whispered. "We only touched once."

"Touched…?" Josie said. She winked. "I have it on good authority he's here already."

That perked me up and I peered around, my heart skipping like he stood right beside me. "Really?"

"Why don't I take the boys for a bit to give you a chance to…I don't know. You could stroll around. Chat with a few friends." She smirked, fiddling with her glossy black hair. "Look for Bruge."

There wasn't anything I wanted to do more, but… "We just got here. I know you want to settle into your new home and relax."

Or she could be interested in checking out the new crop of warriors. So far, Josie didn't appear interested in any of the Suthen Clan males. The clans would gather together for the next few months. Perhaps Josie would meet someone who sparked her fire this winter. So far, almost half of the twenty women who came to Ferlaern had found love and mates. Every one of them was a maelstrom bond, meaning they were pretty much soulmates.

"It looks like Savvy has picked out a house for us already." She nudged her chin forward to a row of husk-covered domits on the right. Savvy stood outside it, waving, but she walked toward us when she saw us staring. "We can take the boys for a while."

Savvy was an angel, jumping in to babysit the little ones without being asked. At thirteen, she still held onto the sweet innocence of youth. I hoped she never lost it.

"Take your time," Josie said, urging me on with a

nudge on my spine. "Meander around. Locate Bruge, then do something spontaneous with him."

My face went hot. "I barely know him."

Savvy rushed over and grabbed Will, who'd started to race back toward the trundier pen. She herded him back to us.

"Go," Josie said, taking Will's hand. "I don't want to see you for at least thirty minutes."

"We don't have clocks or watches," I pointed out. "I won't know how long I'm walking."

Her lips curved up in a sly smile. "Then you won't be late."

"Ben? Will? Pay attention to Josie," I said sternly. If they listened, it wouldn't last long. I tapped her arm. "I promise I'll be back soon." If I tracked down Bruge, he'd probably introduce me to his gorgeous mate. Wouldn't that be my luck?

"Where goin', Mommy?" Ben asked, his eyes wide and timid as he took in the Ferlaern striding past us. At seven-feet-tall, they towered like trees over my sons who were small for their age. The tops of their heads barely came to a Ferlaern's knees.

"I'm going to take a walk," I said.

"I wanna walk, too!" Will whined, straining against Josie's hold.

"We'll go out and stroll around later," I said. "Right now, Mommy's going to take this walk alone."

"That's right, boys," Josie said. "Mommy's going hunting."

Savvy snickered and took Ben's hand.

I rolled my eyes and left them, striding toward the center of the village. Ferlaerns strode every which way, armed with various weapons jutting from the leather straps encasing their chests. Sometimes, it felt like I walked into an alien version of Conan the Barbarian as they were universally buff and gorgeous from the horns to their gleaming tusks and their segmented bronze skin. I was partial to their long black hair shot through with purple, as well.

"I will walk with you?" a Ferlaern male coming from the opposite direction asked, stopping beside me. He poked his chest. "I am Saldarn, and I seek a mate."

"Um, err… That's nice of you to offer, but I'm just…" Think fast. "I'm looking for the bathroom." Actually, where was the bathroom? "I don't have time to talk."

"I see." His gaze darted to a domit with a marker dangling on the wall outside. They used the same symbol in the mountains.

Yay, there it was. "Thank you anyway," I called out as I hurried to the domit.

"I will wait?" he asked, following me.

"Nope." I flicked a hand toward him and picked up my pace. "You go on with whatever you were doing."

He frowned as he stuck to my side. "You did not tell me your name."

"It's Alexa and I…" I pushed the door flap aside and hurried into the cool interior, leaving Saldarn on the path. The flap closed behind me, and he sighed. If I were in luck, he'd leave while I used the facilities.

Ferlaern bathrooms were amazing, really. They used a large, round plant and while someone on Earth might find the idea gross, the plant seemed to enjoy…poop. Pee, too.

I flipped back the rounded top covered with smooth spikes and didn't look closely at the jagged teeth deep inside the rounded creature.

"They don't bite," someone told me when I first saw one.

"They volunteer for this job," they also said.

It must be true because they were everywhere.

I hung out with the poop-eating plant awhile, just to give Saldarn time to get bored and leave. Before exiting, I peeked around the door flap, relieved not to find him waiting.

Scooting back to the path, I continued walking through the village until I reached the end, where I turned to survey the neat row of buildings under construction. Was Bruge somewhere among the building crew? As warlord of the Nulet Clan, he must be busy getting everyone settled. It wasn't easy to plan and renovate a village to accommodate hundreds of Ferlaern plus an almost equal number of trundier. Durran told me Bruge was one of the first to arrive, that he would finish off many of the homes himself.

I swung wide around the last few buildings and walked along a big, rutted path leading upward, though I couldn't see over the rise. Steaming mounds of something I didn't want to examine closely speckled the path. I wound around the mounds, continuing toward what looked like a flat plain at the top. My heel caught on a rut, and I paused to wiggle my shoe free.

Yuck. Had I stepped in… Well, I didn't know what kind of poo it might be. The gooey kind. Pausing, I lifted my foot to examine the bottom of my shoe.

Hoarse bellows from above made me stiffen and spin to face that direction.

A herd of giant ostriches with unicorn heads and horns charged this way, their solitary horns slashing back and forth. Their wings flapped but it didn't appear as if they had the strength to fly. Their two cloven feet sent clods of dirt and dung winging out behind them.

I froze, unsure if I should run back toward the village or dart to the side.

The lead beast bore down on me. Red rage blazed in its eyes.

Before the creature could trample me, someone raced toward me. The Ferlaern male swept me up and dove toward the edge of the path.

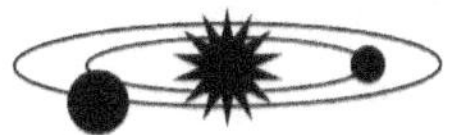

Bruge

The thunder of narlesk hooves drew my eye. Each cycle, the Osten Clan drove a herd to the lowlands. The beasts provided milk to make cheese, meat if our hunts went poorly, and the Ostens often rode the big creatures across the plains.

As it was nothing unusual to see them, I started to turn away. But movement in front of the herd caught my eye.

My jaw dropped.

I'd hoped to find Alexa soon, but I never expected to see her standing frozen while a narlesk herd roared toward her from the hill above.

With my hearts in my throat, I ran in her direction. Would I reach her in time?

I didn't stop, didn't care one bit if I was hurt; all I could think of was saving Alexa.

With the narlesk herd bearing down on me, I swept her up and dove to the side of the trail, taking her with me. We hit the ground hard, and I curled around her to keep her from harm.

She yelped but clung to the leather bands strapped to

my chest. The maelstrom mark on my right shoulder heated, and I muffled a groan that had nothing to do with slamming into the ground.

We came to a stop with her lying on top of me, her legs straddling my hips. If only we were naked, and she was in this position with excitement filling her eyes.

"Bruge," she said breathlessly.

"Here you are, Alexa." Why had I said that?

Blinking, she huffed. "Yes, here I am."

She watched the herd pass before turning back to me. A smile bloomed on her face, sucking the air from my lungs. I could barely think when she looked at me this way.

If I rolled her over and rose over her, what would she do? I wasn't sure I should try. The last thing I wanted to do was offend her.

"Thanks for saving me from the… whatever those things are," she said.

"Narlesks," I said gruffly. "The Osten Clan."

"The narlesks are the Osten Clan?" Humor shone in her voice. "I hadn't heard that."

Why couldn't I think or speak correctly?

"They, um…The narlesks belong to them," I finally said.

"So, the Osten Clan is the group I need to lodge a complaint with?"

I swore she teased. Maybe.

"They drive them here each cycle," I said.

"I thought they were going to run me over."

The would've gored her first. My hearts grew cold at the thought.

The light faded from her eyes, replaced with worry. She nibbled on her lower lip, and I couldn't drag my eyes from the arousing sight.

My cock tightened, the culier strands elongating. My body ached to pleasure hers.

"I guess I should get off you," she said, though she remained where she was. She paused and blinked, and the darkening of her eyes suggested she felt my body's response to hers. It would be hard to miss it as I now possessed a solid bar jutting against the front of my pants.

"You can remain here if you wish," I said.

"You're a guy. With a woody. Of course you'd say that."

I nodded, and my tail coiled around her waist, teasing her side. "Or, if you'd like, you could let me up."

"That's it, then?" Tease came through in her words. "Your woody will fade, and we'll pretend it never happened?"

"Oh, it happened, Alexa."

"It did, huh?" She cocked one of her thinly haired brows, and her body wiggled with mischief. "What are you going to do about it, then, Bruge?"

"Abduct you."

4

Alexa

I must've heard him incorrectly. "Did you say abduct me? Why?"

If this situation weren't so odd, I'd laugh. I mean, I liked him. He had a hard on, which was a good sign.

Which...had to be uncomfortable. Impractical. Exciting.

I wanted to get to know him better.

"How does abduction come into any of this?" I asked.

"I, uh..."

When we first met and shared the infamous brief touch, Bruge said almost nothing to me.

We'd returned to that moment again.

Shit. Did he dislike me? Maybe that was why he wasn't talking.

His hard on suggested otherwise...

"Why would you want to abduct me?" I asked again. Heat flared between us, and it felt wonderful, but we needed to get a few things straight between us. Abduction was out of the equation.

"Ferlaerns abduct females."

Something had been lost in this conversation. No one had mentioned abduction before. "You don't plan to abduct and sell me, I hope."

He growled. "Never."

"Then why do it?"

"It is our way," he said gruffly.

"I see." I didn't, but he was a male of few words. "Back on Earth, when guys wanted to do something with women, they… do some sort of sporting activity together. Go on a picnic. Or if they're truly inspired, they take a painting class together. Abduction doesn't come into that equation."

His thick brow ridge wedged together, making his bronze, segmented skin scrunch. "I do not know these tasks."

And I was assuming his abduction comment implied a date. Maybe he meant something totally different. Our cultures spanned two opposite sides of a wide river, and I couldn't quite make out the other side.

The tip of his tail teased up my spine. Something undefined and exciting flared between us, and it felt wonderful. So did sitting on his body. His cock twitched again between my legs, the thick length pressing against me.

I was in this for his mind, however, not just a bout of hot sex.

Although—

"Bruge," a male Ferlaern said, striding over to stand beside us. He blinked as he looked down at us but said nothing, which was funny. How often did he chat with Bruge while a woman sat on top of his cock?

Ugh. Please tell me this wasn't a regular occurrence. He wasn't one of those guys, was he?

With irritation driving me, I scrambled off Bruge and stood opposite the warrior.

If he'd been interested in me, he would've found a way to make it known, correct? The fact that I'd been on this planet for months without seeing him didn't speak well for my hopes of some sort of relationship with him.

My ears went hot as mortification set in.

"I'll see you guys later?" I said brightly as Bruge levered himself off the ground.

"Could you wait a munette?" he said, his gaze scanning my face. He frowned as if he didn't like what he saw there.

It wasn't easy looking pretty all the time, buddy.

If his friend weren't here, I'd say it to Bruge's face.

"I have information about the duskhorde," his friend said, his gaze studiously avoiding me. "But I see *this* Earthling is here. If you need help with your plan to—"

"No!" Bruge said before continuing in a more reasonable tone. "No. I do not need help," he groused.

Help with what? Probably something related to the duskhorde. A shiver tracked through me. When I closed my eyes, I could see them rushing toward us with a predatory gleam in their fiery eyes.

"If you change your mind…" the Ferlaern flashed his tusks and slapped Bruge on the shoulder. "I am happy to assist."

"I do not need assistance with this."

"It did not appear so. How did you talk her into—"

"What were you saying about the duskhorde?" I asked, studying the other male. They all had inky black hair shot through with purple, but this guy's purple was almost pink. Fuchsia, I guess you'd call it. Back on Earth, few men would be caught dead with hair this color, but this guy pulled it off.

He was a few inches taller than Bruge though Bruge's shoulders were a tad broader.

The two males exchanged a heavy glance before Bruge

mumbled something that could be a Ferlaern swear word. He better not say it around my sons. They'd pick it up and run with it, shouting it at the top of their lungs.

"This is my friend, Zetar, of the Osten Clan," Bruge said, flicking his hand toward the other male. "As you surmised, Zetar, this is Alexa Evans."

At least he was speaking in complete sentences now. And he remembered my last name.

Zetar dipped his head my way.

"Nice to meet you," I said.

Zetar didn't wear a powldron, the leathery shoulder shield fused only to warlords. It supposedly boosted their strength. Since he didn't wear one, Zetar wasn't a warlord. Was he a leader like Garek before the powldron claimed him, elevating him to warlord status? Leaders had to fight each cycle to maintain command of a Clan. A warlord was a lifetime appointment.

But, no. Bruge said he was a friend so perhaps he was one of the warriors in his Clan.

"The duskhorde tribe continued into the mountains, though they skirted around our villages first," Zetar told Bruge. "As I thought, they took the passage to the upper plains, perhaps to join with their northern tribes."

"All of them took the passage, or did any…leave the horde as they traveled through the mountains?" Bruge asked, squinting in the bright sunlight.

"None left the horde," Zetar said.

"Good." The tension riding Bruge's shoulders loosened. "Could you set up regular winged patrols? I want to watch them."

"Here or also in the mountains?"

Bruge scratched the back of his neck. "I hate being unaware of their movements. Enlist a flight of warriors for longer patrols, covering the area as far as the first mountain valley. If they return this way, we'll see them before they reach the plain."

"All right," Zetar said, nodding slowly. "I have a few warriors in mind for this task." His gaze fell on me again, his eyes sparkling. Why was he laughing? "Are you sure you do not need help with—"

"No," Bruge barked out.

"If you change your mind," Zetar said. "I have ideas."

"I said I can handle this."

Bruge studiously avoided looking at me. What was this about?

With a dip of his head my way, Zetar departed, striding toward village. Beyond it, the herd who nearly ran me down mingled in a pen, behaving as if they hadn't been about to kill me.

"Will more giant unicorn ostriches be coming in from the range?" I asked.

Bruge raked his fingers through his hair. "Range?"

Funny how he ignored *unicorn ostrich* and focused on *range*. And there I went deploying some of Piper's "new wild west" terms. During our journey from Earth, she kept saying she wanted to build a new wild west on Ferlaern. Our initial settlement didn't work out, but we molded the idea to fit with the summer Ferlaern lifestyle in the mountains. We'd hosted a square dance and held regular karaoke, though the latter really wasn't wild west. It was just fun.

"Range means..." I tapped my chin, watching numerous emotions flit across his face. I couldn't read a single one. "I guess it means the plain." I swept my arm toward the long stretch of wavering grain beyond the village. "I assume in your spare time, you're cowboys herding unicorn ostriches on the range." From the way he grazed the tip of his tusks across his top lip, it was clear I wasn't making any sense.

But the gesture was hot.

"What are…boys of the cow?" he asked.

I nodded in the direction where I left Josie with my sons. "Walk with me, and I'll explain."

He grunted and fell into step beside me.

I told him about Piper's plan. "In the original wild west back on Earth, humans would ride beasts out to the range and drive herds of cattle into the town and secure them in pens."

The flash of his tusks made my heart skip. "We do something similar. Go out to the…range. We bring in the narlesk herd and hold them here for the winter."

"Do we eat them?"

"Rarely. We milk and also ride them."

"Now that sounds cool. Your trundiers are glorious. I might try to bond with one next summer, but I wondered if you had ground transportation."

"We use them to hunt warslette." He snapped his tusks together. "They are much tastier."

"We should host a barbecue, then." I was warming to the idea already. I had my own new wild west dreams to fulfill, just like Piper. Was there a haymow I could roll around in with Bruge?

"What is this Q of the barb?"

"It's a way of cooking big slabs of meat over an open fire. We could make barbecue sauce. Corn on the cob and pie. Lots of pie." My belly rumbled, reminding me it needed me to fill it. In the mountains, we gathered in community domits—the Ferlaern word for building. Everyone took turns cooking, and we ate together. "On Earth, I worked at a bakery." On Ferlaern, I made flat things out of compressed leaves that were supposed to be similar to pancakes. They weren't.

"You cook?"

"I make a decent cake, if I do say so myself. I can't wait to test out some of the recipes I'm adapting to fit with Ferlaern ingredients."

"I like to eat," he said gruffly.

Sounded like a match made in heaven.

We reached Josie's domit, but when I scratched on the door flap, she didn't call out from inside. I didn't hear my boys in there, either, which was unusual. They'd napped almost the journey today. By now, they should be wreaking their usual havoc.

"Josie?" I called, expecting her to come flying out of one of the other single-story cornhusk homes with my boys in tow. With a flushed face and frazzled hair, she'd hand them over and politely tell me she didn't believe she could watch them again. Only Savvy stuck it out more than one round.

Speaking of Josie's daughter. Savvy came running from where we left the trundiers. She sported the flushed face and frazzled hair I expected from Josie. Instead of exasperation, complete terror filled her face. It woke an answering fear inside me.

"You've gotta help," she said to Bruge, rushing over to us.

"Is everything okay?" I asked as her panic transmitted itself to me. It swept me up and made my heart slam against my ribcage. "Where are the boys?"

Tears sprang up in her big brown eyes eyes. "They took off on Bindy, the female hatchling I was working with."

I would've fallen if Bruge's arm hadn't swept around my waist, holding me up.

"Tell me what happened," I said, struggling not to shriek. My boys. No!

"It was only a second, but they were gone and…" Savvy choked on a sob. Tears streaked down her light brown face. "We ran after them but they're quick. They jumped onto Bindy, and she winged into the sky."

5

Bruge

A lift of my hand, and three of my warriors came running.

"Two younglings have taken a trundier," I said, my gaze scanning the sky. I didn't see them, but that meant nothing. "In what direction did they fly?" I asked Savvy.

She pointed to the west.

"We'll take a small fleet and find them," I told my warriors.

"I'm coming with you," Alexa said, stepping forward with determination in her stride.

"We'll travel faster without you."

"I can ride my own trundier."

I frowned. "You bonded with one?"

"No, but…there must be a free one I can use."

"All are bonded with others and will not…" I bit back my growl. "All right. You can ride with me."

She gave me a pert nod. "What supplies should I bring?"

"I'll get them." I gestured to one of my warriors, and

he pivoted and ran toward my domit. He'd know what we needed and would pack enough for her as well.

"Tell your mom we'll find them and bring them back," Alexa said, latching on to Savvy's arms. "It's not your fault. I don't blame you a bit. I know my boys." Her voice faded to almost nothing, and her eyes swam with tears. The two females hugged. "My boys. My little boys. They're only three."

"I'm so sorry, Alexa," the youngling said. "It's my fault."

"It's not, Savvy." Alexa took Savvy's hands and squeezed. "It's my boys. They do what they please. Too often."

"I vow we will find them and bring them home safely," I said, hoping I could keep this promise.

"Bring Bindy back, too?" Savvy said, her voice cracking. "I called and called, hoping she'd hear me and come back but she didn't."

Alexa stepped away from her and wiped her eyes. "We will."

Zetar and Kunde ran toward me, tossing me a pack as they passed. I took Alexa's hand and we jogged toward the trundier herd, where I directed her to my mount, Nykas, and helped her onto his back.

A cry from the village made us turn in that direction. Savvy ran toward us, pointing toward the sky.

Alexa tipped her head back and sigh of relief eased from her lungs. "It's Bindy. Bindy's back. My babies are safe!"

We all relaxed; happy this was almost over.

But when Bindy landed, her spine ridge was empty.

6

Alexa

I was gutted. My sons were lost, and I had no idea how to find them.

"A group of us will search the ground," one of the Ferlearn warriors said grimly. Without another word, he pivoted and ran toward the enclosure holding the narlesks.

The expression on his face lingered in my mind; he thought my sons had fallen. That they were dead.

They were gone from me forever, just like my poor husband.

"We wing," Bruge said, jumping up onto the trundier behind me. With his arm snug around my waist, he nudged his heels against the beast's sides, and the creature leaped from the ground.

Within seconds, we soared above the long plain of wavering grains. Four other warrior mounted trundiers spread out around us to cover a broader area.

"We will swoop one way then the other," Bruge said by my ear. "We won't miss anything below us."

It was a good plan. Why did the thought of finding them on the ground crush me?

I was stupid to come to this planet. If I'd remained on Earth, they'd be safe. The words kept spiraling in my mind, dragging me down, down along with them.

"It's not your fault," Bruge said softly. He leaned to the side, his gaze intent on the area below us. I looked as well but saw nothing but endless, wavering stalks of grain and a few ostrich unicorns grazing.

The wind whistled past us, whipping my hair into a frenzy. I should do something with it, maybe tie it back, but all I could think about was my sons. Were they hurt? I could almost hear them crying for me.

"They're good boys," I half sobbed. "Sure, they're a handful at times, but they're just kids. I do whatever I can to protect them." Maybe too much, sometimes, but I lost my husband. The thought of my children following him shred through me like giant claws.

"You are an excellent mother."

"Yet here we are, searching for my lost sons." Tears welled in my eyes and were snatched away by the wind. I tried to look for Will and Ben, but it was hard to see when my eyes swam with dread.

"We will find them," he said. "We'll bring them home. And then we'll watch over them. We'll keep them grounded until they are ready to take to the skies. I promise you this."

He sounded so certain. I wanted to grab onto his words and hold them tight, but they kept slipping through my fingers like barbed wire, flaying me wide open.

"Thank you. I feel stupid that I let this happen."

His arm tightened around me. "Never stupid. You're brave, strong, and cunning."

I snorted through my tears. "Why do you think that?"

"Look at you, traveling so far with your family. You came to my world unknowing of what you'd find here.

That's true bravery. And you're strong. You ride on my trundier without fear in your heart—"

"You shoulda seen me during my first flight."

"I wish I'd held you for your first flight."

His words shouldn't make me think of him and what might be growing between us. Not while my sons were missing. But they made it easier for me to lean back against him. They made my heart slow to a more normal rhythm.

It was vastly different riding with Bruge compared to the older, fatherly Ferlaern who transported me from the mountains. Bruge's embrace was comforting. Soothing.

Stirring.

Fire licked along my bones.

"Your strength shines in your eyes," he said.

"Good thing, because there's not a speck of it in my body right now." I lifted my arm and clenched it to show my lack of upper arm muscle. "I used to work out, but that kind of fell by the wayside."

"Strength of will outmale strength of might."

Outmale. Outmale? Oh, like *outman*.

"So says the supermale Ferlaern," I said. "You guys outmuscle, outweigh, and outheight us. I know the last isn't a word, but I imagine you know what I mean. Look at you. You're a warlord, the master of your clan. You're brave and strong, and I don't imagine anything messes with your mojo."

"I think *you* do."

My heart skipped. "I do what?"

He didn't say anything for a long time as he continued to scan the ground. I looked but only saw a variety of creatures, from slender deer-like things to the lumbering ostrich-unicorns. And birds. Lots of birds of varying sizes, flying, and perching on scruffy trees and rocks. Seeing so many wild creatures made me worry my boys might have survived a fall only to be eaten.

Don't do that.

"You mess with my...mojo," he finally said. "I don't completely understand the meaning of the word, but my translator says... a magic charm, talisman, or spell, which cannot be what you mean. I believe you're suggesting something else."

"Mojo, yeah. I was saying you come across composed and assertive, but it's innate within you. I don't imagine anything messes with your world."

"And I just said *you* do."

"Why?" I had numerous "why" questions, actually. Why was he saying this—now? He had all summer to visit me in the mountains, if he was interested, but he hadn't.

Yet maybe he was but had other things he had to take care of. And why did I find that notion exciting? Well, I knew the answer to that, but still.

He snorted. "You ask why you choose to mess with my world?"

"You know what I mean."

His arm tightened around me, and his voice dropped to something low, gruff, and sexy. "You mess with...things just by being you."

"I don't know if that's good or not." I practically held my breath, waiting for his answer. "Maybe lay it out for me."

"I—"

One of the other Ferlaern flew in close to us. "We're going to split up to cover more area."

"Good idea," Bruge said. He pointed forward. "We'll continue in this direction. They had less than an hora, and the trundier's a youngling still, though she's sprightly. Keep that in mind for distance."

The male nodded and peeled his beast away from us and to the right. Another flew left while the remaining warrior split off and urged his trundier back toward the village, perhaps to continue beyond, in the opposite direction.

"The odds aren't good," I gulped out, my eyes filling all over again. I was going to sob until I found them. If they were okay, I'd sob while I scolded them then cling to them even more than I had since their father died.

I didn't dare imagine not finding them safe.

"Don't give up yet," he said. "I haven't."

He sounded so sure, but Savvy's trundier returned empty. Unless she flew down and they hopped off, they'd fallen. Hell, they were probably dead! My heart seized and I didn't know how I'd go on without my boys. They brightened my life. They made me laugh. Without them, my world was empty.

Pain ripped through me. My arms were so empty.

We flew for about twenty minutes, Bruge studying the ground to the right, me to the left. The plain went on forever, dotted with numerous creatures.

"Are there predators out here?" I asked, gnawing on my lower lip. It would be raw soon, but discomfort there might pull a bit away from my heart.

"The zathers hunt the narlesks," he said.

I shuddered as my imagination took flight. "There's a creature that can hunt down and kill the ostrich-unicorns?"

"Zathers are rare, fortunately. They seek narlesk eggs before they hatch and then they go after the hatchlings. Much like the liscards in the mountains, who hunt the trundier young. Zathers don't often attack a mature adult, though if one is injured, they're easier prey."

"My sons are small." Too small. They took after me, not their tall father.

"I have not seen a zather yet," he said, though we both knew that meant nothing. My sons weren't here, either.

"I assume zathers have fangs, claws, and they're the size of a trundier."

"Not quite."

Something new to fear in this world. This was why the Ferlaern were huge, survival of the fittest. Small Ferlaern would have a harder time fighting off the vicious creatures in this world. "Do zathers come near the village?"

"Not often."

Which meant they did. If, and this was a big if, my sons survived, and I brought them back safely, I'd watch them like a hawk. They loved to sneak off on adventures together. Back home, with my fenced-in yard, that meant scooting underneath the drooping branches of the willow in the back corner. Or huddling where the wooden fence met the house. Exciting places to them but with little danger outside a tick or bee sting.

Here, my sons would be hunted by zathers.

"What else?" I asked, squinting at something ahead. Two specks moved along the ground, but they could be anything. From here, they were small enough to be the deer-like creatures. But hope bloomed in my heart, expanding to the point it pinched. I couldn't catch my breath. Please, let it be them. I pointed. "Can you fly your trundier in that direction?"

"Ah," Bruge huffed out, leaning forward.

"Is it them?"

"I... Maybe?" With his knees, he guided his beast to the left and then straight, aiming for the specks that kept moving. Running, actually.

When we got closer, my heart swelled, bruising against my ribcage.

It *was* my boys.

They wailed as they darted across an open, barren plain.

A giant, cat-like creature raced after them.

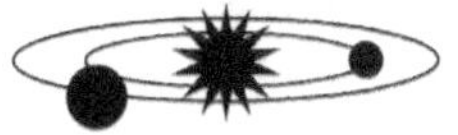

7

Bruge

zather. Of course. Rage surged through me.

Cunning and fast, zathers sought the weakest. Two youngling males without claws, horns, or a tail, would be easy prey.

But a full-grown Ferlaern warrior mounted on a winged trundier would not.

"Hold on," I hissed to Alexa as I urged Nykas down. My arm tightened around her waist, pulling her against me, and her hands wrapped around Nykas' spine spike.

Nykas knew what I needed, because he spiraled, building speed as we approached the ground.

Alexa's soft gasp was sucked away by the wind. She released the spike and clung to my arm as I kept her safe within the shelter of my arms.

"Will. Ben," she said through gritted teeth.

Fire coursed through my veins, giving me the strength of ten Ferlaern. As Nykas approached the zather, I took Alexa's hands and placed them on the trundier's spike again.

"Hold this," I said. "I'm going to…"

Nykas pulled up before he slammed into the ground, leveling off a male's height above the wavering plain. I pulled my short sword and as we passed the zather, I plunged off Nykas and onto the beast's back.

The creature snapped around, a snarl rumbling in its chest. It gave up its chase of the boys and, loping in a broad circle, tried to buck me off. I clung to its spine while my tail wrapped around its belly. With my heels digging into its furry sides, I hefted my blade and plunged it down quickly. It deflected off the creature's thick coat, to the side, and I bit back my groan.

The beast ground to a halt and whipped its head and body forward, trying to send me flying across the sharp spikes jutting from its snout. I clung, knowing if I fell, my chances of landing and bringing up my blade in time were slim. Once a zather sensed a kill, it was relentless. I had to finish this now or this zather would end me. It would eviscerate me and eat me alive.

Then it would track down and kill the defenseless younglings.

Nykas landed a short distance away, and Alexa slid off my mount. She ran to her boys and grabbed them, lifting them off their feet. She ran to the other side of Nykas.

Nykas stomped his feet. He arched his spine and tipped his head back, shrieking loud enough to make a weak male's heart stall. Claws ripping into the ground, he loped toward the zather. Trundiers hated zathers almost as much as they despised the liscards who also hunted their hatchlings.

I gouged my blade forward, seeking the creature's spine. Nykas could be fierce in battle with his claws and teeth, but trundiers more often took flight rather than remain behind to battle. They were safer in the air than anywhere else.

My sword struck true, digging into the creature's neck. It reared back, trying to unseat me, but I whipped my tail forward and wrapped it around the creature's neck. My legs tightened on its sides while I shoved my blade deeper. I hit something vital, and blood squirted from the wound.

The beast stumbled forward, dropping to its knees. It groaned, and a wheezing sigh huffed from its lungs. It wasn't dead yet, and its claws and tusks could rip a male apart in a flash.

Nykas' tail whipped out, hitting the zather's head, knocking it sideways.

I flung myself off the creature, leaving my blade buried in the beast. After a quick roll, I rose to a crouch while pulling two knives from the straps on my chest.

The zather skittered and ran toward Alexa and the boys. I bellowed in fury and gave chase as Nykas flew up and landed between them. He bared his teeth and shrieked. The zather lowered its head, its long horns jutting forward to impale my trundier.

I ran with all I had and drew abreast of the zather. With a shout, I whipped my arm out, slicing my blade across the beast's neck. It shuddered, and its pace slowed.

It toppled forward, stumbling onto the ground in front of Nykas.

The trundier reared back and brought his trunk-like front legs down onto the creature, ending its life. Nykas danced on the carcass, and it shuddered and bounced.

"Bruge," Alexa cried, racing around Nykas with her boys still clutched in her arms. She ran up to me and set them down, giving each a look that would make even a grown male hold still. "Are you okay? You're not hurt, are you?" She strode around me, inspecting me from all angles before stopping in front of me. Her hair hung in a tangled mess around her shoulders and sweat coated her flushed face.

I'd never seen anyone more beautiful in my life.

"I am unharmed," I said. After cleaning my knives on a tuft of grass, I returned them to their sheaths and did the same with my short sword after removing it from the dead zather.

Returning to Alexa, I stooped down in front of the younglings and gave them a stern look. There were many things I wished to say but first, I held out my arms.

They rushed forward and I gathered them close, giving them the comfort and shelter of my body. Tiny things, I could pick them up and stride around with them if I chose. It was the same with Alexa.

How could such small beings have captured my heart—hearts—so quickly? The mark on my right shoulder—the maelstrom mark that proved I was as much Alexa's as she was mine—stung. I nudged a leather strap aside and gaped as two tiny specks blazed in the center before fading to small starry dots. I'd never heard of anything like this happening before, but the fates had a way of pushing us down their own path. The stars were for Will and Ben.

Alexa rubbed their backs. When her eyes met mine, something wonderful blazed there.

I hoped a speck of her joy was for me.

Nykas continued to stomp on the zather, turning it into a bloody pulp.

"Enough," I said, though kindly. My friend had run to my defense, and I owed him special treats when we returned to the village. He adored fruit that grew on trees close to the river, and I'd fill a basket for him. Alexa's younglings could help me feed it to Nykas in exchange for my trundier's service.

He huffed and spun away from the zather, though he

remained nearby, his intent gaze scanning the vicinity. With him around, nothing would come close.

"What happened?" I asked the boys.

They pulled out of my embrace but remained close, each keeping a hand on one of my knees.

Sensing no other threats nearby, I sat and patted my thighs. The younglings clambered up onto my lap, each taking a side, and stared up at me with tear trails forming on their dusty cheeks.

"Bindy bad girl," one of the boys said. Identical, it was nearly impossible to tell them apart.

Alexa sat on the ground in front of me and released a heavy sigh. "I don't imagine Bindy begged you two to jump onto her and take flight, Ben," she said dryly.

Ah, so Ben was the one with a tiny scar on his right hand. Will was the other youngling.

The relief in Alexa's posture and on her face made my hearts fill to overflowing. I was grateful I could give her this, her boys safe and secure.

"Bindy really bad," Will said, looking up to me as if he expected me to jump in to support his comment.

"You left Savvy and went to Bindy," I said, prompting them.

"Big trundy call us," Will said, flinging his arms up overhead. "Ride. Ride!"

"Ride," Ben whispered.

"She didn't beg you to ride," Alexa said.

Will squirmed. "Savvy mean."

"You mean Savvy wouldn't let you go near the trundiers," Alexa said, her brow narrowing. "And you ignored her."

Ben joined Will in squirming, wiggling so much, he nearly fell off my lap.

"Trundy big and fun," Will said.

"Really fun," Ben added.

"I well understand the lure of trundiers," I said. "Did you know I bonded with Nykas when I was four-years-old?"

"You didn't," Alexa said, her eyes widening.

Her fingers pressed against her lips, and I couldn't help wondering what it would be like to tug them away and replace them with my mouth. She would taste sweet. She'd set my veins aflame. But I couldn't do something like that around her younglings.

"I can't imagine a small child riding a trundier," she said. "I'm nervous enough for Piper now that her eight-year-old son, Noah, is bonding with one. He'll be flying within a year. Missy, Rayne's daughter, too."

"It is common. Many of us bond early, though there is still a chance for those who are older. Like you, if you wish."

"Oh, I haven't decided about a trundier."

"You needn't make up your mind this munette. Each summer, more will hatch, and you can go to the nesting grounds and see what happens." I shot a fond look toward Nykas. "Look what my friend just did, helping me defeat a zather."

"I'll think about it." Her gaze grew stern. "Back to you two," she said to her boys. Her hand latched onto each of their arms as if she needed to hold onto them to assure herself they lived. It looked like she'd never let go. "You got onto Bindy, and she took flight. Tell me what happened next."

"High in da sky!" Will said, pointing up to the clouds.

"Scary," Ben said with a nod. "High."

"You didn't fall," she said.

If they had, they wouldn't be alive.

"Big kitty. I wanna pat him," Will said with a soft

moan.

"Back to Bindy," Alexa said, studiously avoiding looking at the zather carcass. "We'll get to the kitty eventually."

The body wouldn't remain here for long. Already, carrion birds circled overhead, their shrill cries bringing in others. We needed to leave this area soon. Zather also weren't opposed to eating each other. A fresh kill was easier than hunting something that might give defense.

"Bindy go wooo!" Will said, his hand diving down toward the scruffy dirt beneath me.

"Big woo," Ben said, demonstrating by lifting off my thigh and falling back down. "Bump."

Alexa tapped her chin, studying them both. "And you two jumped off when you were close to the ground."

"Bindy scary," Will said. "But kitty scary, too."

"Mean kitty," Ben said solemnly.

And thus, we pieced it together. They snuck away from Savvy, got onto Bindy—somehow—and she took flight. She landed and they jumped off. The zather must've frightened her as she took flight again and returned to the village, leaving the boys behind.

"The mean kitty won't hurt you," Alexa said. Tears swam in her eyes again, and when they met mine, I read stark desperation there. "You're safe now, but you have to promise you won't get on a trundier again without an adult present."

The younglings said nothing.

"Boys?" Her voice lifted. "Promise."

"Okay," they said in unison.

They were young and full of adventure. I doubted they'd be able to hold that promise for long. We'd have to reinforce it.

Which gave me an idea…

8

Alexa

"We're walking back to the village rather than flying on Nykas," Bruge announced.

"What?" My gaze flew to the trundier who appeared unharmed. Maybe he was injured while pulverizing the… giant kitty? I couldn't think of it as a kitty. I loved cats and could snuggle with them for hours.

Nope, this was an alien saber-toothed tiger. With six legs and a long, spiked tail. Horns. And claws as long as my forearms.

A shudder ripped through me. If we hadn't gotten here in time… The image of my boys being ripped apart kept flashing through my mind.

"I'll send Nykas back with a message," Bruge said.

"Hold on." I held up my hand as he pulled one of his smaller knives from the armament on his chest. "Why are we sending Nykas back with a message?" An ominous feeling swept through me.

"As I said, we will walk back."

"Like… Walk, walk? It's a long way home." I scanned the area where a billion zathers could be lurking. Birds bigger than my sons circled overhead, eager for us to leave so they could feast.

"Consider this a Ferlaern tradition, one similar to those on Earth," he said with a flash of his tusks.

"Getting stalked by other zathers?"

"You mentioned sports. Walking is a sport, is it not?"

My lips thinned, though he had a point. "It's dangerous out here."

"There is danger everywhere." His attention darted past me but when his posture loosened, I didn't turn to look. He dropped down in front of my sons and pulled two small knives from the armaments on his chest—if six inches long could be called small. He held them out hilt first. "One for each of you."

Ben's eyes widened.

"Whoa," Will said, snatching one from Bruge's palm. He backed up and slashed it back and forth, nearly lacerating his brother.

"No knives," I said, stepping forward. "They're dangerous."

"Every male—and female—must be able to defend themselves." He tugged another blade from his endless supply and held it out to me. "Even you, my precious female."

A tiny part of me (okay, a big part of me) gushed about the "my" and "precious" parts of his comment, but weapons were serious business. "They'll trip and fall and gouge themselves."

"We won't, Mommy," Will said, flicking his blade back and forth. "This is fun."

"Fun," Ben said, latching onto the other blade with a ruthless vigor. He snarled and shoved the blade up into the sky. "Cut kitty."

"Why are we not taking your trundier back to the

village immediately?" I asked, feeling flustered and not from the thought of my boys carrying blades, the dead carcass nearby, or the big birds circling overhead.

This world was big. Overwhelming. The thought of being out here alone made my blood turn to stone.

"This adventure wouldn't be much of an abduction if we rode back, now would it?" Bruge said with a light in his eyes that called to something wild penned up deep inside me.

"What abduction are we talking about?" I asked.

He flashed his tusks in a grin. "The best kind." Turning, he leaped onto the trundier's back. After tossing his bag onto the ground, he secured a scrap of cloth to the creature's spike.

"Okay, so we're walking back," I said, resigned. I ignored the tingles inching up my spine. Damn, Bruge was sexy. I wanted this kind of stuff turned my way, but not when we were out in the middle of nowhere and not while my sons watched avidly.

I wanted to spend time with Bruge, even if that involved abduction, but that didn't include battling vicious beasts with a knife. Where was a tank or rocket launcher when you needed one?

"We are," he said.

It wasn't far. Just ten or a billion miles. At least I wore sneakers, jeans, and a t-shirt, as did my boys.

I squinted up at Bruge. "Everyone at the village will know what's happening from a scrap of fabric alone?"

"This says everyone's safe, that there is nothing wrong. They'll know we found the younglings, and we're making our way back by other means."

His gaze fell on the boys slashing their blades through a tuft of tall grass. Severed grain tops flew everywhere. The knives cut through the stalks like butter, and a shudder rippled through me. Ben and Will were going to cut themselves; I just knew it.

"I'd like to work with the younglings a bit, if that's acceptable to you," Bruge said, sliding off his trundier. His hand rested on Nykas' chest, and he spoke in the creature's ear. I'd seen others working with their trundier hatchlings, and the beasts had an uncanny way of understanding whatever their bonded Ferlaern said.

"What do you mean, work with the boys?" I was more curious about this than anything else. Well, the abduction comment made me pause as well. But a long walk, I could handle. A knife in my hand only improved the idea. But my sons... They missed their dad. He'd been gone long enough I worried he'd become a distant memory for Will and Ben. "I know I cling to them, maybe more than I should. I'm often too lenient. Everyone tells me that. You have to understand. They're all I have. I'm all *they* have."

Bruge approached me, scooping his bag off the ground as he passed it. He leaned in close to whisper by my ear. His nearness made my soul quiver. "We Ferlaern teach younglings like your boys how to survive in the wild. We start when they can barely walk."

Focus, Alexa.

"They're only three-years-old." I was skeptical about this. "I don't mind if you want to talk to them. We need to lay down the law and make them understand they can't ever do anything like this again. But what purpose will walking back do? It'll take us hours—horas, that is—to reach the village." If we made it today. My sons didn't mind a short walk in the park, but miles?

Creatures could hunt us while we did it.

"Horas. Yes, exactly," he said, strapping his bag onto his back. "Do you trust me?"

"Yes, but..." Frankly, it was hard to think with him this

close. He smelled awesome, like fresh air and male. His scent heated my pheromones up and made them flounder around inside me. It wasn't fair. I felt frazzled and sweaty, and I was sure I smelled after riding a trundier all day to reach the village. We hadn't bathed this morning before we left camp. Or yesterday, for that matter. My pits must reek. *I* must reek.

Meanwhile, he was Mr. Cool, Calm, and Collected. Not a trace of sweat. Not a trace of stink.

He studied my face before nodding, but I really hadn't given him an answer, had I?

Walking back to Nykas, he held the creature's snout while the beast huffed and snorted. When he stepped back, Nykas took flight. He circled over us before heading toward the village.

A slopping sound made me turn to find Will and Ben gouging the bloody carcass with their knives.

"Boys," I groaned, starting toward them.

Bruge held me back with a tap on my arm. "Allow me?"

I shrugged. "Sure." I should be stomping over and making them behave, but I was tired. Twins could be over-whelming, like they were magically four kids getting into trouble instead of two.

"Younglings," Bruge said, and the boys jumped, proving they knew they were not supposed to be smacking the bloody remains. "It's time to leave."

"Where Nyki?" Will asked, peering up at Bruge. At just over three-feet-tall, the top of his head came to Bruge's mid-thigh. Really, the Ferlaern towered over all of us, even me at five-six.

"Nykas has flown back to the village," Bruge said.

"Wit-out us?" Ben's head tilted. "I wanna go home." Tears welled in his eyes, and his bloody knife dropped from his hand. He scampered around Bruge and raced over to me, almost knocking me over when he collided with me. He hugged my legs. "Wanna go home, Mommy."

"We are going home, sweetie," I said, rubbing his back. I tried to inject enthusiasm into my voice, but it was hard. "We're going to walk to the village."

"Nykas bad boy." Will glared at the sky and shook his knife. "Nykas! Come back!"

Nykas was long gone and would not be returning no matter how loudly Will berated the trundier.

"Come on, Will," I said, holding out my hand. "It's going to be fun walking back to the village." Probably not, but I'd become a pro at putting on a happy face no matter how much grief or fear overwhelmed me.

Will frowned at Bruge then held out his hand toward the Ferlaern.

Bruge took it and with a flash of his tusks my way, walked around the steaming beast's remains to join me and Ben.

"Carry," Ben said, holding up his arms toward me.

I started to stoop down as Bruge reached us.

"We are *all* walking," Bruge said, tugging Ben away from me, though gently.

Ben jutted his lower lip out. "Mommy carry me."

Actually, Mommy had a feeling now might be the time to follow Bruge's example.

"We're all walking," I said lightly. "That means you, too, Ben."

He dropped to the ground on his knees and burst into tears.

Will's eyes filled as he watched his brother. He clung to Bruge's finger as the tears trickled down his face.

"We will walk for half an hora, younglings," Bruge said

cheerfully. "*Then*, we will carry you." He strode toward the village, tugging Will along with him.

I looked from him to Ben. "If you sit there crying, you won't get back home."

"Carry, Mommy," he said with a pout, his tears miraculously drying.

"You need to walk. Bruge said half an hora and half an hora it will be." Bruge wasn't the only one who could draw an invisible line and stick with it. "I won't carry you until then."

Ben flopped back onto the grass and kicked his feet, his arms flailing.

I didn't want to leave him. After all, big birds circled overhead, waiting to feast on the zather remains. My son was too small to defend himself against them, despite the knife he still gripped in his hand.

On the other hand, I shouldn't give into his demand and carry him. If nothing else, I tried to stick to something once I stated it.

"It's going to be lonely here alone," I said.

"Carry me!"

My spine stiffened. "No. You will walk half an hora."

"Benny," Will cried from twenty feet or so ahead of us. "Come on. You can do it!"

That was my Will, always cheering on his brother. They were close as twins could be, but Will somehow intuitively knew he was the elder, if only by a few minutes. He led while Ben followed.

Ben sat up. "Wait fa me!" Scrambling to his feet, he bolted after Will and Bruge, his little legs churning.

So much for being unable to walk. Hefting a sigh, I followed.

Half an hora lasted about twenty minutes before the boys started whining.

They were tired. I got it. We rode on trundiers for days and with the power naps while we winged toward our destination, making their nighttime sleep restless. It wasn't easy sleeping on the ground, though the Ferlaern gathered what we Earthlings called memory foam leaves for us to lay on.

But walking, we would do.

At least Bruge found a trail about two feet wide that meandered through the deep grass. I trailed my fingers along the grains as we walked, speculating about how edible they might be. On any other day, I might enjoy this.

About when I deemed it was time to give up and give into their demands to be carried, Bruge stopped.

"Who would like to ride?" he asked brightly.

"Me," Will shouted, jumping around Bruge with more energy than I could drum up on a good day.

"Me, me," Ben said, holding up his arms to Bruge.

"I can carry you both." Bruge shot me a grin as he stooped down. "If I am going to hold you, however, you need to remain still and hold onto my horns. No stabbing me with your knives and no dropping them, either."

"Cool," Will sighed, squinting up at Bruge's head. "I want horns."

"Me, too," Ben cried. "Mommy, where my horns?" He prodded his head as if he hoped to find nubs.

"I'm afraid you won't be growing any," I said. "Humans don't have horns." Which was kind of sad, actually. On Bruge, they made him appear imposing. Gorgeous. From his black hair shot through with purple to his bronze, segmented skin, he was one hot Ferlaern. The first time I met him, I developed a crush. It hadn't relented all summer, despite the lack of contact between us.

Bruge hoisted Ben onto one shoulder and Will the other. He straightened and started marching toward the village as if he carried nothing. My boys weighed in at about thirty pounds each, per my guess. Without scales, it was hard to know for sure.

Funny how important all those measurements were when we lived on Earth. Here, kids grew as their bodies chose and no one worried if someone didn't add another more inch to their height before a certain date.

We had no doctors here. Ferlaern healers took care of wounds, and they were well-versed in local diseases. If we got sick, I guess we could communicate with Earth. Or go see Josie, who'd worked as a nurse back on Earth.

The lack of traditional medical care should stress me out, shouldn't it?

I wasn't sure why it didn't.

Maybe because we put our lives into fate's hands when we arrived here. Whatever happened, happened. We'd deal with it then.

We walked for hours, and the sun slowly sunk toward the horizon.

In the distance, something gleamed, and as we approached, I spied the river.

"We'll follow it to the village?" I asked Bruge.

Ben and Will leaned against his head, their hands clinging to both his horns and their knives, their eyelids drooping.

"We will, though we will not reach the village until the next sunslice," he said.

I peered around, wondering how long it would be before we ran into our next threat. I saw plenty of options when we flew over this area.

"We're spending the night here?" I whispered, trepidation creeping through me.

"We will."

"We'll be safe?"

"Of course."

I frowned but continued to walk right behind him. My footsteps slowed, however, as I was tired. Like the boys, I kind of wished I could nestle against Bruge and take a nap. If I begged, would he give me a piggyback ride?

When he stopped, I smacked into his back.

"Oh, sorry," I said, shoving the hair off my face. Really should've thought to bring an elastic.

"We will camp here tonight," Bruge said pleasantly.

He didn't look winded, which wasn't fair. Meanwhile, I felt like I'd competed in a triathlon. Sweat trickled down my spine, and my heels were kicking up a protest.

Bruge led us closer to the river and stopped in a small clearing. He lowered my boys to their feet, one by one, and they drooped on the ground, sleepy.

"No resting," Bruge said as he slid his pack off and tossed it onto the scruffy, tamped down grass. He shot me a quick flash of his tusks before smoothing his face. "It is the males' duty to hunt for the females."

Talk about chauvinistic.

"I can hunt," I said. Not really, but someone needed to speak up for womankind. "Where will we hunt?"

"In the river."

"Fishin'?" Will asked, getting off the ground and jumping around, restored after his power nap.

"Fish, too!" Ben said, joining his brother in their jumping bean competition.

"We got poles?" Will glanced around then frowned, his shoulders drooped. "No poles."

"You don't know the trick?" Bruge said with a twinkle in his dark eyes.

"Teach me," Will chimed in.

Ben latched onto Bruge's leg. "Me, me!"

"Come to the river, younglings. Your mother will start the fire while we're gone."

I wanted to grumble about the little woman hanging back to get the stove going, but while I did not know how to fish, I did know how to start a fire. I'd gotten plenty of practice while traveling from the valley where we originally hoped to settle to the mountains and then from the mountains to the plains.

"Sure, don't mind me," I said blithely, rolling my eyes. Maybe I wanted to learn how to fish, too.

I snickered as I headed up a narrow trail parallel to the river, picking up sticks and dry brush that I knew from experience would burn well. After I gathered kindling, I'd find larger pieces. I'd make sure I gathered a lot, as I wanted to keep the fire going all night long to keep predators at bay.

Ugh, predators.

Maybe this "walking to the village" idea wasn't so hot after all. I'd yet to see it teach my sons any sort of lesson. I didn't like the idea of us out here alone all night.

Returning to the clearing with my load of wood, I tossed it onto the ground. I located a decent pile of rocks and made a circle in a sandy location, then stacked the kindling, stuffing dried leaves among the sticks. Then I trooped back upstream to gather large pieces of wood.

Meanwhile, it looked like the guys were at a pool party. They stood thigh-deep in the water. Thigh-deep for my boys, that is. The current just licked the bottom of Bruge's knees. Will and Ben kept splashing each other while Bruge watched the water.

They had no fishing poles, and I had a sad feeling my belly would be rumbling this evening.

Until one of the boys squealed and Bruge grunted. He hefted a fish a little more than two feet long over his head and tossed it onto the shore while the boys squealed and jumped around.

Were there more fish that size in the river? My sons were in there!

I started in that direction before making myself stop. Bruge would watch out for them. He'd never put them in danger.

"I really am a helicopter mom," I whispered.

Making myself turn away, I walked upriver, collecting wood.

By the time the boys had snagged two more fish, though I assumed Bruge caught them all, I'd collected a sizeable pile of wood, enough to see us through the night.

As I added more wood to the pile, the three males sat by the fire ring, cleaning the fish. Even my boys attacked the sides of a fish with grisly determination, their knives slashing out, their faces knitted with concentration.

"Take care with your blades, younglings," Bruge said, sitting between them, watching. "You don't wish to cut yourselves."

"I won't," Will chirped.

"Won't," Ben echoed softly.

"After we've removed the scales, we need to gut them," Bruge said.

"Cool," Will sighed. "Guts."

I'd seen my share of gory things since arriving on Ferlaern, but I was glad they were completing this task and not me.

"Do you have fire rocks?" I asked Bruge, nudging my head toward the pit. "I'll get it started."

He handed them over, and I stooped down to click them together. Sparks flew, and the soft, dry brush caught fire. Perfect.

I straightened. "Why don't I collect some tubers to go

with our meal? I saw a nice crop of them growing along the shore." They tasted vaguely like potatoes, and I'd learned how to dig and cook them since arriving on Ferlaern. I was proud of the new skills I'd gained since I got here. Each fed my belief that I would not only survive here if I were somehow separated from the others, but that I could also feed my sons.

There was something wonderful about knowing you could "live off the land".

"Tubers would be a nice addition to our meal, don't you think, younglings?" Bruge said.

"Yeah!" Will said, diligently scraping scales off the fish. Ben echoed the word, though his scraping lacked Will's feral enthusiasm.

"You're doing very well, younglings," Bruge said, watching my boys with pride, as if he was their father teaching them a new skill.

Did he want a place in our lives?

He acted sweet and kind, and my heart jumped around whenever he came near, but I wasn't sure of his feelings. He might just be acting friendly.

As I walked toward the river, I wondered how I could find out.

I dug a bunch of tubers and was contemplating stripping and wading into the water for a quick, private dip, when I heard a stick snap behind me.

My heart thumped faster, and my skin crawled with fear.

I spun as a four-legged creature sprang from the bushes and galloped toward me.

Horror bolted through me. I backed up, tripping over something.

I fell into the water.

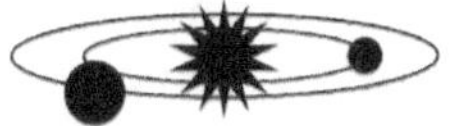

9

Bruge

A sound from the river made my fingers still on the fish. I set it aside and stood.

The younglings looked up at me with matching frowns on their faces.

Unease crept up my spine, and I learned cycles ago never to ignore this feeling.

"Where we goin'?" Will asked in excitement, tossing his partly cleaned fish onto the leaves I'd collected to encase them for steaming.

For Ben, the thrill of gutting fish fled after the first slice. He gulped and tears welled in his eyes. After that, he refused to do anything further. I would work with him, show him he could do this, but in a gentler manner. In my world, being able to gather food and prepare it could mean the difference between life and death. Younglings learned skills like this from the time they could walk.

Will had dug into cleaning his fish with a slashing eagerness I almost envied.

"I wanna go. I wanna go somewhere!" Will jumped up and hopped around me. Ben watched me with speculation, showing me he was as clever as his brother, if not more so. Will was full-on with everything, dashing into things without thinking them through. Ben practiced caution. Many might dismiss him because he hung back and was quiet while his brother drew all the attention, but not me.

I was the same at that age, letting my older brother shine while I waited for someone to notice I could contribute, too.

Now my brother was dead from a duskhorde attack, and I'd stepped into the role he'd prepared for from before I was born. The powldron was never meant for me, but I would do my best to live up to everyone's expectations, especially my mother's.

"Don't wanna taka walk," Ben said. He crossed his arms on his chest and thrust out his lower lip. "I'm hungry. Want hot dogs wit ketchup."

"Earthlings eat...dogs?" The word translated to a small, loyal beast Earthlings kept as a pet.

"Yucky," Will said, his face twisting. "We don't eat dogs, silly."

"Yes, no dogs, hot or cold," I said. "Tonight, we eat fish."

"Don't like fish," Ben said, his eyes filling.

"You're going to love this fish. We'll cook it ourselves." I kept my voice light, though unease continued to pick at my spine. Alexa should be back by now. "I need to check on your mother."

"Where Mommy?" Ben asked, looking around.

"She went swimmin'." Will said, his churning legs taking him away from the fire, toward the river. "I wanna go swimmin' too."

"She didn't," I said, grabbing onto the back of his shirt. I tugged him back and deposited him beside Ben. "She went to the river to collect tubers. They taste like...

hot dogs. With keech-up." Whatever that was. My translator was no help, suggesting this was some sort of bloody liquid. Surely Alexa didn't feed her younglings something like that.

"Wanna go swimmin'," Ben said. "I's hot."

"Not now." I shook my head and looked around, hoping I'd see Alexa returning to us. "In the morning."

"She's tubin'. Don't wanna go tubin'." Will sat down again and grabbed his fish, flopping it over. "Yucky scales."

"You boys either need to come with me or hide," I said, itching to race to the river.

"Hide and seek?" Will chirped. "I wanna play."

"I don't mean that kind of hiding," I said, not wishing to frighten them. I needed their cooperation. The chance of anything threatening them while I was gone was slim, but I didn't dare risk it. "You must come with me to find your mother or hide."

"Come on, Ben." Will sighed and dropped his fish again, maintaining a tight grip on his knife. "We's gotta hide."

Ben looked around, bewildered. "Why?"

Will held out his hand. "We's gotta."

Ben got up, shooting a concerned look from me to the path leading toward the river. "Want Mommy."

I cupped his small shoulder and squeezed reassurance. "I'm going to get her, and then we'll eat dinner."

"Come on," Will said, leading his brother into the deep grass. About three Ferlaern's length in, they sat and disappeared.

"Don't come out unless I call," I said, striding toward the path.

The munette they could no longer see me, I broke into a run, eating up the ground with my feet. I'd held in my concern with the younglings, not wishing to frighten them.

Now, as I raced toward the water, I let my fear consume me.

I snatched weapons from the sheaths on my chest and a low growl rippled through me.

Reaching the river, I peered around feverishly.

"Alexa," I called out, low and urgent.

A snorting, huffing sound pulled me to the right, and I raced up the trail, coming to an abrupt stop when I spied a small clearing.

Alexa lay on the ground with a half-grown droog mauling her face.

I leaped forward and shouldered it off her. It tumbled to the side and yelped as it landed hard on the ground. Scrambling to its feet, it flung itself over her, where it pivoted and growled at me.

"Get off me, you doofus," Alexa said with a gurgling laugh. She gently nudged the droog to the side and sat up. "Oh, hey. Bruge. How's it hanging?"

I blinked slowly. Hanging?

"Do not move, and I will kill it," I said, taking a careful step forward. Almost as large as she was, the droog could rip her throat out with one twist of its head.

"No way," she said, jumping to her knees and wrapping her arms around the beast's neck. "No hurting this sweet pupper."

"That is a vicious creature."

The droog licked her face.

"He's not vicious. Don't hurt his feelings." She pouted and rubbed the droog's head, her fingers sinking into its ruff. Leaning forward, she kissed its snout. I had to admit, a spark of jealousy lit inside me. What would it be like for Alexa to treat me with this much affection?

I'd determined to abduct her and seduce her like Ferlaern did long ago, but so far, my plan wasn't turning out as I intended. I hadn't exactly abducted her, and even if I could call us walking back to the village an abduction, I couldn't seduce her with her younglings around.

And now she appeared to have befriended a droog.

"It is a wild creature," I said, striving for patience. She was new to Ferlaern. She didn't understand our ways or rules. I would teach her like I did the younglings, and she would learn.

"He's just a big snuggle bunny, aren't you?" Her arms tightened around the droog's throat, and she leaned back, tugging him down on top of her again. They wrestled in the grass while I fretted.

"Droogs are not friendly," I said, despite the creature nuzzling her throat. "And it is a she." The beast was softening Alexa up before ripping her apart.

"Okay, *she*. And she is friendly." Alexa wiggled out from underneath the beast and got to her feet. The droog leaned against her side and gazed up at her with complete adoration.

I was sure I looked at Alexa the same way.

I'd lick her throat, too, if she asked.

"You must leave the droog here," I said. "We need to return to the fire."

"Why? You know, there are few things I'd ever ask someone for." She paused, thinking. "I mean, a day at a spa would be nice, though that's impossible. Maybe a day to wash my hair and lounge in a tub without little ones interrupting. But dogs? They're a girl's best friend, don't you know that?"

I did not understand what she spoke of. Lounging in tubs? Washing hair?

Her head tilted, and her mood sobered. "By the way, what did you do with Will and Ben?"

"They are hiding in the grass."

"Okay," she said slowly, staring toward where I left them. "We need to make sure they're all right. I never leave them."

"On Ferlaern, younglings learn to hide on command from the time they can walk. They also learn to remain silent so as not to draw in a predator. We have tricks we teach them from a young age."

Shadows filled her eyes. "Oh, yes, predators." She scooped up a small sack lumpy with tubers and hurried down the path.

The droog cocked one eyebrow at me before huffing and bolting after her.

I sighed and followed.

A droog was not a pet. They did not live in our village. My warriors would kill it on sight.

But when it leaned against her as she walked, and she buried her hand in its ruff, my hearts sighed.

If she wanted to keep it, I'd find a way.

We reached the campsite.

"They're not here," Alexa said, her tone lifting with a tinge of panic.

"Younglings?" I called in a low voice that would only carry as far as the grasses. No need to draw in zathers. "You may come out now."

Will stood and squinted toward us. "Whoa. What's that?" he asked, rushing toward us.

Ben poked his head up. "A doggie!"

He scampered after his brother but the two stopped half a male's length away from the droog.

"Mommy, how come da doggie has six legs?" Will asked, his head tilting.

"Because it's a Ferlaern dog," she said.

"Wanna pat the doggie," Ben said with such longing, my hearts pinched tight. "Can I?"

"Of course you can," she said, stooping down beside the droog. She looped her arm around its neck. "Come close and let her sniff your hand before you touch her. Remember, this is a wild creature."

I grunted, feeling somewhat vindicated.

Will barreled over but skidded to a stop and jutted out his hand for the droog to sniff. I hoped it sniffed and didn't bite.

The Ferlaern avoided droogs; we didn't befriend them.

As if it sensed my hesitation—or saw my hand tightening on the hilt of my short sword, the droog dropped down to its belly and whining, wiggled toward the youngling.

Ben held back, watching his brother. But when Will tumbled down beside the droog and laid across its back, cooing, Ben came forward.

"Always wanted a dog," he said.

I frowned. Did he think this was a hot dog?

"How would one put kee-chap on this...hot dog?" I asked.

Alexa tipped her head back to look up at me. "Ketchup?"

Ben promptly burst into tears. "We not gonna eat him!"

10

Alexa

O nce we'd assured the boys we would not eat the droog, they settled down beside the fire.

We soon had the fish steaming in thick, moist leaves, and the tubers roasting in the sack. The air smelled so good; I could almost eat it.

Without ketchup.

"This droog needs a name," I said, my hand still buried in its soft ruff. Will and Ben hadn't left the creature's vicinity.

Bruge sat rather forlornly on the opposite side of the fire, watching us with a hint of longing in his eyes.

"Why don't you come over here?" I said, patting the ground beside me.

He jolted, and his eyes blazed when they met mine.

It was a simple suggestion. I didn't intend to grope him. But answering heat swirled inside me, totally inappropriate with my boys around.

"It is nearly time to eat," Bruge said. Standing, he tugged one of the leaf-wrapped fish off the low coals, peeling back the top. Steam lifted from the opening, and my belly rumbled at the amazing smell. I couldn't remember when I last ate.

"It is done," he pronounced. He pulled the other fish and the bag of tubers off the fire then carefully peeled back each leaf to dump a few tubers beside each fish.

Will rocked forward, fidgety. "I'm hungry for fish."

"Me, too," Ben said softly. He leaned against the droog. "Love doggie, Mommy."

"Do you want to name her, Ben?" My son had begged for a dog from the time he could talk.

"Me?" he asked, his face alight with joy. It made me realize how often I responded to Will's outgoing personality but didn't try to bring out the slower response with Ben.

"Yeah, name her." Frowning, he tapped his chin. "What it gonna be?"

Bruge placed one of the fish in front of me and the other near the boys. He tapped the droog's nose when it started inching toward the fish. "Not for you."

"She hungry," Will said.

"You eat first, and she can have what's left," Bruge said. "Males are mighty warriors. We need strength to fight."

"Yeah," Ben said, staring up at Bruge in complete adoration. "Gonna be warrior. Gonna be this big." He spread his arms wide.

"Only if you eat fish," Bruge said, flashing his tusks at me.

My belly swirled with heat, and I had a feeling he sensed it because his eyes smoldered. Where was a babysitter when you needed one? The droog did not count.

Will and Ben dug in with a gusto, scooping up big bites with their hands, squealing with excitement when one was too hot.

I couldn't believe how much they ate. Fresh air would do that, my mother always said. That and running for their lives.

As I nibbled my fish that was flaky, lightly spiced with an herb Bruge pulled from his bag, and carrying a hint of smoke, I fretted about my boys' future.

Back on Earth, I pictured Ferlaern as a utopia full of fresh water, clean air, and little to no danger. Since we arrived, we'd been attacked by a fearsome tribe of brutal aliens, the duskhorde. Our supplies burned and we were forced to move in with the Ferlaern. Even that life was no paradise. Creatures hunted the forest and would be as happy to eat us as any other prey.

Now we'd moved to the lowlands and already, we were attacked by a saber-toothed tiger. Well, the alien version of one.

What was next?

Actually, I didn't want to know what might come next.

One thing was clear. I sighed. My boys did need to learn how to defend themselves.

I continued eating the fish and tubers, my belly finally relaxing.

"I will teach them everything they need to know," Bruge said as if he read my mind. His hand strayed to his shoulder, and I frowned. Did I see a mark hiding along the edge of a weapons' strap? It was hard to tell in the low light.

Night had fallen and only the stars overhead and our fire kept me grounded.

"You're busy," I said. "You're the warlord of your clan. I'm sure you have too many responsibilities already to take on teaching my boys Ferlaern life skills."

"I will do this if you permit it."

"I... They need to learn, but..."

"But...?"

I squirmed as it hit me. Damn, I clung to my children as if they were still infants. On Earth, a three-year-old would never be expected to learn how to fight to the death. But on Ferlaern, a lack of training could mean the difference.

"Okay," I said but held up my hand before he could speak. "If it's okay, I'd also like you to train me. I know nothing about self-defense."

Bruge dipped his head forward. "I would be happy to teach you."

"Done," Ben said, shoving the leaf holding less than half the fish away. He lifted his hands. "Need wet nap, Mommy."

I chuckled. "No wipes here, honey. We need to wash in the water."

"Yay," Will said. "Swimmin'."

"No swimming. Just washing your face and hands. Then it's time for bed."

"I will gather bedding while you take the boys to the river," Bruge said. A frown filled his face. "Take the droog with you."

"Who still needs a name, Bennie," I said as my boys got to their feet. "We can talk about it as we walk to the river, which... Bruge, how will we see to get there?"

He pulled something from his bag and held it out to me. "Take this."

"It's moving," I said, staring down at the round, ball-like creature in his hand.

"I should hope so."

"Is it a gerbil?" Will asked, rushing over to see. "Oh, flashlight."

"Wanna see gerbil," Ben said, inching closer.

"It's not a gerbil," I said. "It's... What is it?"

"A clecare," Bruge said. "Watch." He stroked the "ball," and a soft glow bloomed inside it.

"Whatsa clecare?" Will asked.

"A type of larvae that provides light when you rub it."

"Cool," Ben whispered, scooting close enough to touch. At his stroke, the clecare glowed brighter.

We left for the river. The droog rose and sauntered behind Ben, sticking to him like the loyal companion I knew she could be. It felt good having a big, cuddly beast by my side while walking in the dim light.

"Can I hold care-care?" Will asked, lifting his hand.

"As long as you don't drop it," I said, lowering it into Will's cupped hands.

"I won't."

"A larva," I said, raking my teeth across my lip as we drew closer to the river. Back on Earth, larvae went through metamorphosis and turned into fish, butterflies, or even tadpoles. I'd ask Bruge later what this creature turned into.

We washed up and returned to the fire, where we watched Bruge feed fish to the larvae. It actually had a mouth. It coiled into a ball when it rested but unfurled to resemble a large caterpillar when offered a few bits of fish. It ate, and when it coiled back up, he returned it to his bag.

The boys lay across the droog—who still did not have a name—sleeping.

"I prepared beds for them," Bruge said, waving to mats of thick, woven grasses lying beside the fire.

"You did that so fast."

"I have created beds like this many times." He swallowed deeply. "I also crafted your domit back at the village."

"Really?" I'd been the sole provider for me and my

boys for the past two years. It was nice to have someone help every now and then.

Where did Bruge see whatever this was between us going, though? He'd treated me kindly, but much like a warlord assisting someone in his Clan, not like a potential mate or lover.

"If you are not happy with it, I will make changes," he said.

"I'm sure it will be fine. Thank you." I rounded the fire and lifted Ben off the droog. "What are we going to call you, sweetheart?" I whispered to the creature, but she only licked my leg.

"No one names droogs," Bruge said. "No one befriends a droog."

"Don't you have pets in the village?"

His thick brow ridges drew together. "The narlesks could be considered pets."

My lips twisted. "You mean the unicorn ostrich combo units? They're not what I'd call cuddly."

He snorted. "Neither is a droog."

I tilted my head to where the droog snuggled with Will. "This looks cuddly to me."

"I will concede that *this* droog is…cuddly," he said with a sigh. "But none of the others are."

Scooting closer to him, I kept my voice low so as not to disturb Ben. "Just so you know, most women are looking for someone to cuddle with."

Heat flared in his eyes—or so it seemed to me. But the flash could just be a reflection from the fire.

His gaze fell to my mouth, and my heart skipped a beat.

Something was changing between us. I sensed an awareness of… I wasn't sure what, but I wanted to find out.

But not while I held my son. I turned and walked toward the beds Bruge prepared earlier.

"Can I carry Will?" Bruge asked softly.

My smile flashed his way. "Sure, that's sweet of you to offer."

We laid the boys on two of the mats and covered them with a thick blanket Bruge pulled from his pack. The mat squished beneath my knees as if the grasses were made up of something resembling cotton.

Two longer mats lay partway around the fire as if the boys were at nine o'clock and the adult mats at noon.

My mind jumped where it shouldn't, to us bringing them close together or, even better, sharing the biggest.

It was foolish to dream of something like that. Despite the flash in his eyes a moment ago and his offer of an abduction—really? —he wasn't treating me as if he saw me as a potential mate.

The droog padded over and settled between the boys and the deep grass. I stooped down beside her to give her a long rub behind the ears. She whimpered and groaned and rolled over, begging for belly pats—which I delivered.

"Aren't you a good girl," I said softly. "Help me watch over my boys, okay?"

She licked my hand and grunted then laid her head on her front paws with a heavy sigh. I understood. Watching my boys was a full-time job.

"Goodnight song?" Will murmured, half asleep.

Bruge looked to me.

"It's just a silly song I made up for them." But, like every night back on Earth and all since we arrived on Ferlaern, I sang it, telling how the birds cheep and the cows moo. And the buzzing bees flit from one flower to another.

"Again," Will said when I finished.

With a deep voice that sunk tendrils deep inside me, Bruge sang the song, not missing a word. When he finished, Will and Ben's soft breaths told me they were sleeping.

My heart pretty much split wide open and let him inside.

"Would you like to sit by the fire before we rest?" Bruge asked in a low voice. "We can still see them from the other side."

"That would be nice." We had no marshmallows or graham crackers for S'mores, but Bruge was better.

I rounded the fire and settled on the ground, and after a moment's hesitation, Bruge dropped down beside me, his thigh brushing mine.

I'd gotten used to how big these guys were. At five-feet-six-inches tall, they towered over me in an almost comical manner. Sitting, the top of my head didn't reach his shoulders.

"Do you feel as if you've settled in well on Ferlaern?" he asked.

"Mostly." I poked the fire with a stick, and sparks flickered up into the sky. The wind had died at sunset, and smoke coiled, swirling through the sparks.

"You don't wish to return to Earth?"

"Not at all. To be honest, I wondered about doing something like that when I first arrived. I can still hear the duskhorde's screams when I close my eyes. I felt fairly safe in the mountain valley, however. Garek's a kind and caring warlord, and he made sure all of us felt welcome." He took particular care with Piper, but she was his maelstrom mate, so that was to be expected.

"And now?" Bruge partly turned toward me to watch my face.

How could I tell him that I'd looked forward to coming

to the lowlands mostly because he'd be there? It felt too soon to say something like that, and I still wasn't certain of his thoughts about me.

"I'm happy here," I said. "The boys love this planet. I can't imagine returning to Earth."

"Will you seek a mate?" His hands stilled at his sides, and I swore he held his breath. Did he worry about my answer?

Now was not the time to suggest *he* could step into that role if he wanted. Instead, I explained about my husband dying from the illness and struggling to raise two infants alone.

"You must miss your mate," he said.

"He was a good guy. He loved his boys."

"And you?"

"At first. We were married five years before I got pregnant, and he stressed about it, worrying he was the reason or maybe it was me. We went to specialists, and he had a low…" It felt disloyal to say this about my husband. "We had a hard time getting me pregnant."

"I'm sorry."

A soft smile filled my face. "Don't be. I have my boys and they're perfect. I'm sorry he's not with us to watch them grow."

Bruge nodded slowly. "Then you will not seek a mate."

"That's not true." I shot a glance his way but couldn't read his face. What did he hope to hear from me? "I came here with the intention of meeting a Ferlaern male."

"Ah."

I dragged my fingertip through the dusty soil by my leg. "Maybe I'm waiting for the right Ferlaern to show me he's interested."

"How would a male do something such as that?" he asked. "Speaking hypothetically, that is."

My shoulders curled forward. Hypothetically, huh? Did that mean he wasn't interested? "There are lots of ways to attract someone you like."

"How would someone attract *you*?"

I turned fully to face him. "What are you saying, Bruge?"

He shrugged. "On Ferlaern, we have specific things we do when we're courting someone. What do Earthlings do?"

"Lots of things."

Maintaining a relationship with my husband became a challenge after testing discovered his low sperm count. He insisted he was deficient, and he worried all the time I'd leave him for "someone with lots of sperm". Then I got pregnant and yay, twins. That seemed to help.

But our relationship felt strained despite the gift of our boys. Something I couldn't define came between us, and I couldn't find a way to break down the barrier. Then he got sick and died, and my chance was over.

I hoped when I came to Ferlaern, I could fall in love again, that I could build a special relationship with someone new. When I met him, I thought that was Bruge.

But what if he had a different Earthling in mind?

"What things should I do?" Bruge asked.

Wouldn't that be my luck to like this guy only to discover he had a crush on someone else. "Is there anyone in particular you'd like to get closer to?"

"There is."

Ugh.

"Who is she?" I asked.

"Don't you know, Alexa?" His voice had gone deep and gravelly. "It's you."

11

Bruge

Alexa blinked at me, her lips parting.

Had I offended her by stating my intentions? Actually, I hadn't stated much, just indicated I was attracted to her.

"What are you trying to say, Bruge?" she said. "Don't beat around the bush."

Glancing around, I frowned. "Why would one beat a bush?"

"It's an old saying." She held up her hand when I started to speak. "Forget the bushes. Tell me."

She wanted confessions, but I wasn't sure how to express my feelings.

I never thought I'd want to be with any of the Earthlings. At first glance, I found them unappealing. But the fluff on their heads and their tiny, curvy figures became familiar eventually and then attractive. And once I talked with a few of them, the wonder in their voices as they got to know my world sparked an excitement inside me. What would it be like to start anew on a planet far from my own?

Then I met Alexa. I hadn't seen my maelstrom symbol

until after she left with Garek's Clan, but I knew she was the one I was destined to meet.

To love.

Did I love her? It was hard to know. A warm feeling filled me whenever she was near. Yes, the maelstrom mate call sparked my second heart and formed the symbol I'd bear for the rest of my sunslices, but it took more than that to bring about love.

I wasn't sure I had time for emotions like that. There was so much to do to keep the village running smoothly. And the duskhorde were an ongoing threat.

"Bruge?" She rose up onto her knees, bringing her face nearly even with mine. Her hand reached up—slowly— and I remained frozen while she traced her fingers across my cheek. Her warmth sunk into me as her other hand cupped my neck.

My breathing raged like I battled five zathers.

I ached to feel her grip my horns while I sunk into the heat between her legs.

The scent of her arousal glided through the air, calling to me. It became my undoing.

I wrapped my arms around her and brought her fully against me. She wouldn't miss my erect cock straining against my pants.

Our mouths came together, and it seemed as if the stars in the dark sky above exploded.

My chest rumbled with my groan, and my two hearts slammed against my ribs, seeking a path leading only to her. The maelstrom mating call urged me to lay her on the ground and consume her, but I'd already learned from my brief interaction with Earthings that females were delicate. They needed to be treated with care, not rushed into a feverish mating.

Alexa pressed herself against me, and her tongue dipped inside my mouth to tease across mine.

Fuck it. I couldn't help it.

My mouth plundering hers, I laid her on the ground and rose over her, a warlord determined to claim his mate. A true abduction could wait.

It was time for seduction.

I traced my fingers along her side, and she arched into me. Her hands tugged at the straps holding my weapons, and I ripped them aside.

"Yes," she said, her hands stroking my chest.

I kissed down her neck to the collar of her shirt and pulled at it with my tusks. I wanted her naked. Beneath me. Now.

As heat roared through me, the culier threads on my cock lengthened and stiffened. Once inside her, they'd stroke her inner walls and drive her to a fever pitch.

I returned to her mouth, unable to get enough.

Releasing harsh pants, she remained locked against me.

I cupped her between her legs, and her moan swirled around us. If I could only touch—taste—her hot flesh.

I struggled with the fastener to her pants but couldn't figure it out.

Her low laugh was followed by a smile that made my cock twitch. She reached between us and not only undid her pants, but she also wrenched them off, as well as the tiny garment beneath.

"Touch me," she commanded, and I had to admit, I enjoyed her aggression.

She latched onto my horns as I moved down her body. The simple touch on a part of me so sensual made flames lick across my bones.

A nudge, and she lay splayed open for my hands, tail, and mouth.

"Bruge," she sighed when I licked her opening, pushing my tongue deep inside. "Yes." Her voice came out in a hoarse whisper, remaining low so we wouldn't be disturbed.

Parting her lips, I stroked my thumb down her slit. Her pearly clit lay revealed to me, and I devoured it with my mouth, carefully gliding my tusks across it.

Alexa moaned and pushed up to meet me.

I slid my finger inside her. Two. Pumping the way I would with my cock.

She brought her knees up and lifted her hips with each of my finger thrusts. Her head thrashed on the ground, and her short, feverish cries echoed around us.

I licked and sucked her clit, savoring her intense satisfaction.

Until she released a hoarse cry and shuddered beneath me.

12

Alexa

I'd never done anything like that before. And with my sons lying around the other side of the fire!

Jeez. What if they'd awoken and came looking for me?

Oh, Bennie, sweetie. I'd say. *Would you mind lying down a bit longer while this alien warlord sucks on my clit until I come?*

With my guttural cries, he'd think Bruge was attacking me, which…he kinda was. With his amazing mouth and his long, thick fingers.

After that, I wanted his cock and everything else he had to offer.

But the situation was enough to give a kid nightmares.

While Bruge rose and fed the fire then checked on the boys—something I as their parent should be doing—I pulled on my clothing.

He returned to sit beside me. "Would you like some water?" he asked, lifting the soft flask he'd filled at the river.

"Sure." And a solid fuck. I wanted that, too. Fingers were all well and good, but they couldn't compare to a thick, hard cock driving inside me.

I hadn't seen a Ferlaern cock yet, but Piper and Rayne hinted these guys were built in more ways than one.

"You will move in with me, into my domit at the village," he said with satisfaction he couldn't be feeling. He hadn't gotten off just because I did, had he?

"That sounds proprietary, Bruge," I said, not committing to anything.

"You said you wish to find a mate. I wish to mate with you."

That got my back up. "Is that all this is? Sex?"

He frowned. "Your sex is female. Mine is male. I do not understand how these terms come into this."

"I'm saying that just because you got me off with your mouth and fingers, it doesn't mean we're shacking up."

His ongoing frown was highlighted by the flames licking across the wood. "I do not live in a shack."

"Domit. You know what I mean. You don't own me."

"I do not wish to own you. I only wish to find you in my bed furs at the end of each sunslice."

"I'll need more than a good finger fuck to convince me I'm yours."

He flashed his tusks my way. "Challenge accepted."

"It wasn't a challenge. It was…" I had no idea what it was. Flustered, I stood. "I'm going to bed. Alone."

I wasn't sure why I felt ornery. He'd given me an awesome orgasm and with one crook of my finger, he'd deliver more. Hell, if I stripped and laid on the ground with my legs splayed wide, I had a feeling he'd devour me until we both bellowed.

But… Maybe I did want a little courtship.

You will be in my bed furs at the end of each sunslice felt…clinical. Boring. A bit too controlling for a woman who'd taken care of herself for the past two years.

"I want hearts and flowers and all that junk before we

do the big deed," I announced, starting around the fire toward the two mats.

I turned to look back at him because he wasn't following.

He just grinned. He knew he had me already.

"When we reach the village," he said. "We will leave the younglings with a friend, and I will abduct you."

There he went again with the abduction talk. I wasn't sure why this was so important to him, but I would go with the flow.

If his tongue, fingers, and cock were part of the package, I was open to an alien abduction.

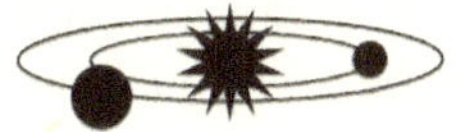

13

Bruge

I was eager to take on Alexa's challenge.

So, she refused to move into my domit, did she?

It was time to show her what she was missing. I'd given her a taste—and tasted her—and now I needed to increase my seduction.

This wouldn't be easy with younglings around, but I adored them and only wished to see them content and happy. Alexa and I would have our chance once we returned to the village.

We laid on our separate mats and Alexa tossed and turned until I tugged her onto mine and held her in my arms.

"This doesn't mean I'm moving into your domit," she groused as her head rested on my arm. Her fingers trailed across my abdomen, and my cock responded, thickening.

"Sleep," I said. "In the morning, I will pleasure you again."

"Overly confident, aren't you?" she huffed. "What if I only orgasm once a month?"

I just grinned. This female responded to my touch completely. I could touch her this instant and she would savor yet another orgasm delivered by me.

"Are you saying you do not wish for this?" I asked.

Her long pause followed. "No. I'm not saying that."

My grin got bigger. I was enjoying her game because we would both win.

"Then you will not mind if my fingers find you before the younglings awaken," I said, gliding them down across her belly.

Her body tightened, but she sighed when I slipped my hand into her pants and stroked her folds.

"Like this," I said. "Tell me you do not want this." I glided my finger into her wetness.

She moaned and hitched her leg up over my thigh. "I'm not saying anything, but…Ohhh."

I growled in her ear, and my cock became the hard, aching length it was not long ago.

Her inner folds squeezed my finger, and I added another one, driving them up into her. My tail coiled around and joined the fun, stroking her clit.

She panted, her lower body jerking toward my hand with each pump. She was sweet and it gave me such joy to make her come.

"Would you like my cock buried deep inside you, mate?" I murmured, savoring her gasps and blunted cries.

"Yes," she hissed. Her body tightened and she moaned as she spasmed around my fingers.

I moved slower, teasing her clit as she relaxed fully against me.

Easing my hand out of her pants, I sucked on my fingers.

"Bruge," she said softly, watching me.

"Yes?"

"You're such a fuckin' tease."

Her breathing slowed and evened out, telling me she slept.

I couldn't stop smiling.

14

Alexa

I had no clue what I was going to do about Bruge. In a stupid fit last night, I told him I didn't want to move in with him.

Maybe because he'd stated it like it was a done deal.

And maybe because my mind was still spinning from the mind-blowing orgasms he pulled from me again with a few simple strokes of his fingers and tail.

I was easy. No doubt about it.

When he growled about driving his cock inside me, I came undone. I couldn't be responsible for what happened after that.

My world was whirling out of control, and I was afraid I'd fall off the edge. I needed to step back and think before leaping all over him.

Assuming I could hold myself back.

I wanted more than sex. I needed affection and companionship and a solid home for my boys. Whatever was happening between us couldn't be solely about sex.

The sun rose, and before the boys woke, Bruge's tail teased its way inside my pants.

I never thought a tail could do something like that.

It stroked me until I was a moaning wreck. Bruge held me while I came apart in his arms.

"Mommy?" Ben asked as Bruge's tail slid out of my pants and dropped to the ground behind him.

"Yes?" I rose, and it was all I could do to walk.

Bruge chuckled.

Damn, he knew just what he did to me.

"I'm here, Ben."

"Sleepy," he said, leaning against me.

"Come sit by the fire, and we'll have something to eat."

"Want cereal, not fish," he said with a yawn.

But when we served it to him and Will, he dug in with the same gusto he exhibited last night.

We ate another solid portion of the fish then tossed what was left to the droog. I'd heard of people eating smoked fish for breakfast in some parts of the world, and my mom was right when she said hunger was the best seasoning, but I'd be glad to return to the village where I could eat pretend pancakes.

And the grain wavering in the light breeze suggested other options… Ideas for my next test swirled through my mind. There were a few recipes I could try with what I could harvest. Once I perfected the dishes, I'd introduce them to the Ferlaern. My friends had already sampled some of my experiments when we lived in the valley and begged for more.

I had a goal when I came here, and it wasn't sex with an alien.

I wanted to start my own bakery.

Sex with an alien would come second. *Come.* Sigh.

"It is time to leave, younglings," Bruge said with too much enthusiasm.

"You're too enthusiastic," I said, twisting my lips as I stared up at him.

He covered what remained of the fire with dirt, flashing his tusks my way. "You are cranky. Not what I expected. Perhaps I need to tease you a bit more."

His tail flicked around him and glided down my arm.

I shouldn't be turned on by a tail. "I'm always sluggish until I've had at least two cups of coffee," I offered as an explanation.

"She cranky," Will said matter-of-factly.

"I am not," I said with afront, but he and Ben just laughed. I guess they knew me well.

"We do not have coffee," Bruge said with regret.

There was nothing even close to coffee on Ferlaern. While I'd gone through caffeine withdrawal months ago, I still longed for the hot smoky-creamy goodness gliding down my throat.

"Narcial has herbs she steeps for tea," he said. "I could ask for some."

"It's worth a try. Hey, you said something about milking the unicorn ostriches?"

He lifted his bag and settled it on his back. "We milk the narlesks, yes."

"Do you think I could have some when we return to the village?"

"Of course. Perhaps the younglings would enjoy drinking it?"

"Yes, I'm sure they would," I said, not ready to share my baking plans until I'd played around with them first. There was nothing worse than presenting something you hoped would taste amazing only to see the other person gag.

"Are you ready to leave?" Bruge asked, striding in close to me. He smelled amazing. I'd come to the conclusion the scent was pure Bruge. If I licked him, what would he taste like?

There went my smut brain again, dragging me into wild scenarios of me and him. Locked together. Moaning.

"Later," he whispered by my ear.

"I didn't say a damn thing."

He fed me a slow flash his tusks. "You didn't have to, mate."

My hands landed on my hips. "I'm not your mate." Damn, I *was* cranky this morning. I couldn't truly blame it on the lack of caffeine. Or the lack of sexual satisfaction. Or him, I suppose.

This was all on me.

"You will see," he said with so much confidence, I wanted to smack him. Or kiss him. Or, fuck, drop to the ground and show him exactly who would be seeing what. I settled for a smirk, like that would teach him.

"I want you, but I want to be more than a warlord's mate," I said as the boys tumbled on the ground with the droog. "I was sucked into my role as my husband's wife then the mother of his children." As I spoke, I put on my sneakers. "He wanted me to quit my job and that meant giving up my dreams. I missed that piece of myself, and I won't give it up again." Especially for another guy who seems to take too much pleasure in telling me what to do.

"As I said, you will see."

"No," I said, trying to sound firm but I couldn't hold back my smile—he was too damn cute, even when he smirked. "*You* will be the one who sees."

"It is time to leave, younglings," Bruge said with his ongoing cheer.

"Don't wanna walk," Ben said. He yawned and leaned against the droog. "She got a name. Fluffy."

Bruge blinked. "You wish to name the droog. That in itself is…unusual. But…"

Ben's lower lip trembled. "Like Fluffy." He buried his face in the creature's ruff and sobbed.

"He's overtired," I said. "We've been on the go for a long time."

I went to Ben and stooped down beside him, rubbing his back. Will stood nearby, his lower lip trembling. When they were tiny each behaved in the same way as the other. If Will cried, so did Ben. If Ben laughed? Ditto.

"I love the name Fluffy," I told him. "It's perfect for our new pet."

Ben lifted his head and sniffed. "Love you, Mommy."

I held out my arms and he tumbled into them, wrapping his little arms around my neck. My eyes teared. There was nothing that could compare to the pure joy I felt being a part of my sons' lives. I was given a precious gift.

"Carry me?" he asked. "I'm tired."

I looked to Bruge which was funny. Of course, my husband and I made decisions together about our sons but since his death, I'd been in charge. Now here I was, seeking another male's input. I wasn't sure how I felt about that.

Maybe I hovered too much. I lost my husband and with so many men dying on Earth, I feared my sons would be taken from me too. They were spared, and I'd never stop being grateful. I clung to them, though, because I worried they would be ripped from me, too.

But I did welcome someone else's input every now and then.

"I think we should walk a short distance and then… Fluffy should carry the younglings," Bruge said.

"Ride her like a pony?" Will asked, hopping around between me and Bruge.

Bruge's gaze sought mine, and I read the confusion there.

"A pony is a small horse. Sort of. Anyway, it's a creature people ride back on Earth."

"Like the trundiers?"

"No wings."

"Oh." He frowned. "Perhaps like the narlesks, then."

"Closer." I straightened and held my hand out to Ben. "You can hold onto Fluffy with your other hand."

"Where da leash?" he asked, looking around.

"We don't have a leash, and we don't need one. She's with us because she wants to be." Which, frankly, was the best way to include a pet in your life.

As if she understood, Fluffy licked my hand.

Bruge held his hand out to Will, who could barely reach the end of Bruge's finger.

The five of us left our tiny campsite and walked along the river, sticking to a trail Bruge said would eventually lead us to the village.

Fluffy stayed with us, proving she was the perfect fit for my growing family.

"Will we have a problem bringing a droog to the village?" I asked Bruge.

"If she remains by your side as we enter, no. You need to be prepared for opposition, however."

"Why?" I stretched my hand out, burying my fingers in her ruff. "She's the sweetest thing." My heart had split open and welcomed her inside already.

"Droogs have been known to attack Ferlaern."

She did have long tusks and vicious-appearing claws. But she'd behaved like a tame pup since she found me.

"I can't imagine Fluffy would do something like that," I said. "I can work with her, teach her to be kind to everyone."

Maybe I did need a leash or some way to restrain her. I would hate to see her hurt someone and vice versa.

"I will help you with this," Bruge said, his indulgent gaze falling on Ben trooping beside me. "It will help if everyone sees how gentle she is with the younglings."

"How long until we reach the village?" I asked.

"Before we hunger for our next meal."

So, a few hours. "You mentioned a domit for me?"

He flashed his tusks. "I have mentioned a few domits to you. While I prepared a home for you and the younglings, my second offer still stands."

To move in with him. "Let's shelve the offer for now and you can instead tell me about the one you constructed for us."

His grin widened, and heat flared through me.

I was shameless. If the boys weren't around, I'd undo my pants.

"We shall see," he said again. He scooped Will up and turning, placed him on Fluffy's back.

"Wanna ride, too," Ben said, hopping around the droog's wagging tail.

"Can she carry both of them?" I asked.

"Let's see." Bruge lifted Ben up behind Will, and he wrapped his arms around his brother's waist.

"Wee!" Ben said, wiggling his butt. "Ridin' pony."

Fluffy shot me a look that said she'd take good care of my younglings.

I shook my head, amazed at how good natured the creature was.

We rambled along and soon, sounds ahead reached us.

"We here," Will cried, lifting his arms overhead. "We here!"

Trundiers shrieked, telling me they smelled the droog. I kept my hand in her ruff, and my heart drummed like a herd of...well, narlesks, as worry took hold. I couldn't let anyone harm her.

We reached the edge of town and a few Ferlaern working on domits paused. Their voices hushed and they watched as we strode down what I decided to call Main Street as it ran through the center of the village with numerous domits on either side.

Beyond the buildings, trundiers rose and flapped their wings but remained grounded. The ostrich-unicorns galloped around their pen, snorting.

So far, so good.

Fluffy growled, low, and deep, but she didn't leave my side.

By the time we reached the middle of the village, a crowd followed us, murmuring. None of my friends were among them, and if there was ever a time I needed a friend, it was now.

Bruge stopped in front of one of the larger domits with smaller bubbles on each side. Did this one have more than one room?

"This is the domit I prepared for you, Alexa," he said, sweeping his hand toward it.

The flap on the front opened, and an older Ferlaern woman stepped out. Her gaze pinned me in place before she frowned at Bruge. "You have returned."

His posture stiffening, he dipped his head forward. "Yes, Mother, I have."

Mother?

Her narrowed gaze fell on me, and I cringed as she took in my dusty clothing, hair in need of a good brushing, and my flushed, sweaty cheeks. Her huff rang out in the silence. "So, this is the one?"

The one what? Funny how she didn't ask a question but made it a statement.

Bruge nodded. "This is Alexa."

"Alexa." His mother barked out my name as if tasting it and finding it sour. She whirled to face me so fast, her tail nearly smacked a youngling Ferlaern male walking behind her.

Her hands flexing, she strode right up to me.

Startled, I stepped backward.

"How dare you?" she bellowed, her nostrils flaring.

Before I could say a thing, her hand snapped out, hitting my face.

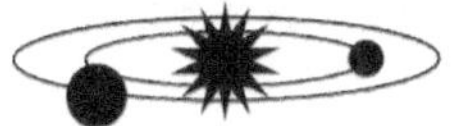

15

Bruge

Alexa reeled backward, gulping. Her hand rose to her scarlet cheek.

"Mother," I snarled, grabbing her arm, and yanking her away from my mate.

Alexa stared at my mother in bewildered horror, rubbing her face.

Anger burned through me, and I wanted to bellow at the female who gave birth to me. She'd done her best to raise me well, but she was not always an easy person to love.

"Mommy," Will cried, flinging himself off Fluffy. He scrambled around to put himself between Alexa and my mother. Reaching down, he scooped up a handful of dirt and threw it at her. "Leave my Mommy alone, mean lady!"

Ben burst into tears and buried his face in Fluffy's ruff.

My mother grunted but only glared at Will. "She needs to control her…" Her hand flicked toward Will.

"What the hell is going on here?" Alexa asked, storming around her son to put him behind her. She gnashed her teeth at my mother.

"Mother, this is Alexa," I said, as if introductions would smooth this hopeless situation. "Alexa, this is my mother, Irella. Mother, you need to apologize to Alexa for hitting her. Now."

My mother's tusks snapped together. "She smells of sex."

A few of the males lingering nearby snorted, but their grins faded when their gazes met with my glare.

"Go back to what you were doing," I told them, turning to my mother. "She is my mate, and you will respect her."

"Mate?" My mother shook her head, and her horns flared red, a Ferlaern female's way of showing anger. "You will mate with a Ferlaern female as I have told you more than once. One who will remain with our Clan. I have arranged for introductions. You will meet the first of my choices this sunslice." With a grunt of disgust, she whirled around and entered the domit, calling over her shoulder. "I have moved into this domit, son. Thank you for preparing it for me."

I internally groaned, knowing my world was about to implode. "Mother. I prepared this domit for Alexa. And you need to come back out here and apologize."

I couldn't force this. Not in front of the gaping village. As the mate of the former and mother of the current warlord—me—she held the community's respect. None would appreciate me sullying her honor, though she did so herself by harming my mate.

Mother poked her head out the door. "She is an Earthling. She is not a worthy mate for a warlord." After shooting a sneer Alexa's way, she let the door flap snap shut.

"I apologize for her," I told Alexa, stretching my hand

out. She avoided it, which was not a good sign. "My mother is wrong."

"About which thing in particular?" Alexa gulped out, her eyes swimming with tears of pain and frustration. I took her hand to tug her close, but she backed away, forcing me to release her. "We know her first accusation is true. As for the last, what if she's right?" Her chin trembled. "While I'm quite willing to find a Ferlaern to mate with, what if that person's not you?"

A growl ripped through me. The symbol on my shoulder proved otherwise but making demands would get me nowhere.

Abduction. Seduction.

I needed to follow this traditional plan if I hoped to win her.

"I will prepare another domit for you," I said. I would not offer mine again. Not yet.

"Thank you, but no." She drew herself up stiffly, and her body shook from unshed tears. "I believe I should prepare my own."

"I will help," Trudar said, coming up beside her. He bared his tusks. "I assume you would like one of the larger ones to ensure separate sleeping quarters for your younglings?"

"I will help as well," Saldarn said, his spine tight as he came over to stand with Trudar. The two males were good friends. "Everyone would be happy to help her, and her youngling sons, settle in one of the better domits."

"*I* will help arrange for another domit for Alexa," I said, feeling as if I was losing something precious. Shifting my weapons' strap to the side, I revealed the symbol to Trudar.

Alexa sent Trudar and Saldarn a tight smile, but her

wince told me pain in her face kept it from becoming full. "Thank you, but…Bruge will help me."

My burning jealousy—which I had no right feeling —eased.

"I see," Trudar said, his lips thinning. He dragged his gaze from my shoulder and pivoting, strode toward the trundier pen.

Saldarn gave Alexa a forlorn look before following his friend.

There were empty domits near mine. Or there had been when we left yesterday. I wanted her near, to protect her. To see her. To show her I was still a worthy mate.

I started to lift my hand but dropped it, not wishing to feel the sting of her rejection again. I nudged my head to the left. "If you'll come this way, I can—"

"Why did you bring a droog to our village?" someone asked.

A large group of warriors from the Nulet Clan shouldered forward, staring at the creature. The low rumble in Fluffy's chest made them pause.

Alexa took Will's hand and they joined Ben, standing between the warriors and Fluffy.

"The droog is a pet and will remain in the village," I said. "Her name is Fluffy." It was all I could do to hold back a grimace when the name was met with more snickers. "You will treat Fluffy with the same respect you give me."

"Until it lunges for one of our throats," someone said from the back of the crowd. "Then it will meet the end it deserves."

"Please don't hurt her," Alexa said, stepping forward. She wrung her hands, pleading. "Give her a chance. She's the sweetest thing in the world. She'll remain with me and my sons in our domit. I promise she'll behave. She will not cause harm."

A few warriors slunk back. They must still hold hope for a potential mating with her and wouldn't wish to give offense.

"It is friendly," I said, reaching toward Fluffy.

The beast stepped backward, baring her teeth. She wasn't angry with me; she must be frightened by the encroaching crowd.

Someone growled, and the droog's fur stood up along her spine.

"Look at it. It's going to attack," someone cried. "Run!"

"No!" Ben shouted, startling not just me, who'd never seen him raise his voice outside of a flash of temper, but a few of the warriors standing nearby. "Leave Fluffy lone!" He tried to wrap his arms around the droog's neck, but his reach wasn't long enough for his hands to meet. When he tumbled forward, landing on the ground in front of creature, everyone gasped.

While a few Ferlaern resisted the Earthlings' settlement, none complained about them bringing younglings.

As one, the warriors drew weapons and stormed forward, prepared to defend the small child from what they perceived as a threat.

Fluffy nuzzled Ben's neck then licked his face.

Ben's giggles chimed out, and the warriors stilled as one.

"Look at that," one said.

"It's going to rip out his throat," another snarled.

"But it's not. Watch!"

The voices merged into a blur of uncertainty and fear. I understood. Our trundiers were wild creatures ages ago when we first bonded with them, but many forgot this and saw them as no more than beasts to ride from one point to another. To see a droog that had always been a threat acting in a loving way with a tiny Earthling must shock many.

Will jumped up, trying to climb onto Fluffy's back, but he was too short.

I lifted him and dropped him onto the creature who turned her head to nuzzle the boy's leg.

"I don't trust it," someone yelled.

I tried to ferret out who spoke, but no one met my eye.

"Do you have more fear for this droog than two small younglings?" I asked.

A few warriors grumbled and turned to weave through the crowd. Others followed, a few shooting uneasy looks toward Fluffy.

Alexa leaned against my arm and spoke, keeping her voice low. "I'm sorry. I've created lots of problems for you."

"You have not."

"Your mother might disagree."

"She is…" Ah, now I understood the term I heard a few times before. "Old fashioned. She lives for traditions."

"I'm not going to come between you two." Straightening, she took a strong step away from me.

My hearts cringed. "What do you mean?" Dread reached out inside me, seeking my vulnerabilities.

"Come on, boys," she said with forced cheer in her voice. "Let's go find Josie and get our things. Then we can find a domit and make it snug from the rain."

"Find domit?" Will asked. He looked back and forth between me and his mother. "What about Bruge? Gonna live wit us?"

"Nope," Alexa said, holding out her hands to her sons. "We're going to live alone like we did on Earth."

Will gazed at me with longing. "What about Bruge?"

Ben nodded vigorously.

"I have my own domit to live in," I said. Again, I would not force this. "But there are open ones near mine."

"Let's..." Alexa sucked in a deep breath then released it. "Give it time, okay? Let things settle, and we can talk."

As she led her sons away with the droog following, I held in my grumble.

Abduction and seduction?

My plan appeared insurmountable now.

16

Alexa

I hated walking away from Bruge. While I was uncertain about him now that his witch of a mother had jumped into the mix, I liked him. A lot.

But I issued a challenge, and I was eager to see what he'd do with it.

As for his mother… Ugh. Who'd want her for a mother-in-law? She'd stab me in my sleep.

"Where we goin', Mommy?" Will asked.

"Goin'?" Ben echoed, looking around.

As we strode to where I believed I'd find Josie, Ferlaern bustled around us, some setting up domits while others planted small gardens along the sides. I was going to have to get going if I wanted even a slight chance of keeping up with the neighbors. Assuming there was an empty domit left for me to claim and then craft a garden alongside.

"We decided we will help," Saldarn said, jogging up behind me with his friend, Trudar. "Bruge is not my Clan warlord. He does not tell me what to do."

Trudar said nothing, but he nodded.

I caught a whiff of…alcohol on them? No, that couldn't be true. There was no alcohol here.

"We will show you the best domits," Saldarn said. "Then we will help you obtain furnishings."

"You will be happy," Trudar added hopefully.

Though my sons on either side of me were in the way, the warriors tried to herd me down the long row of domits.

Feeling a bit uneasy, I came to a stop so fast, Trudar bumped into me.

"Don't rush me," I said sharply.

The boys glanced from me to them, and Ben's lower lip trembled.

Will looked ready to head butt Trudar, which wouldn't do. They meant well, but I would control where my body went, thank you very much.

"Please," I said in as kind a tone as I could muster. "Bruge said he would be along to help me, and I've agreed."

"Where is Bruge, then?" Trudar asked with lifted brow ridges. "I do not see him here, showing you available domits and pointing out the best features."

Good question, but Bruge said he'd help me, and he would. I trusted him.

And while Trudar and Saldarn were offering their assistance, I didn't know them. I'm sure they meant well, but the last thing I wanted was to lead two males on. I wouldn't consider them as mates.

"He'll be along soon," I said. Maybe.

Jeez. I hated doubting him, but my face stung, and I wasn't sure where we stood, if anywhere. Oral sex and a bunch of finger and tail fucks didn't mean commitment.

"We can take you to the best domits," Saldarn insisted. "And then, perhaps, we will talk about your basket and how best to—"

Basket? I had no clue what he was talking about.

"I said no," I barked out, then lowered my voice. "I'm sorry. If I've given either of you the impression I'm interested in a relationship, you're mistaken. In fact—"

"You're back!" someone cried behind me. Josie, Rayne, and Piper rushed toward me, their faces beaming.

When they reached us, Piper gave me a big hug. "So glad you're safe!"

Rayne rubbed my arm. "We were worried."

Josie stooped down and opened her arms. The boys barreled into her, nearly knocking her onto her butt. "I was so worried about you two!" She released them and straightened, fiddling with her hair. "I'm really sorry. We only turned away for a few—"

"No, please," I said, jumping in to reassure her. "We're talking Will and Ben here. These things happen."

I turned to tell Trudar and Saldarn I was all set, but they were striding away. It was for the best. They needed to kiss up to the available women in our group and look at me as taken.

Which… Maybe I was?

Sighing, I turned back to my friends and hugged Josie, whispering. "I'm not upset with you at all. I'm just grateful they're okay."

"We got Bruge's message." She eased back, her face smoothing. "Well, the guys got his message. I was just relieved to hear everyone was okay."

"We all were," Rayne said, and Piper nodded.

"Savvy's been a wreck," Josie said. "She feels responsible."

"Poor kid. I'll talk with her. I don't blame her at all."

"Thank you," Josie said with tears shimmering in her eyes.

We hugged again, our embrace dissolving into laughter. My friends meant everything to me. I wouldn't want them thinking for even a second that I didn't care.

As she stepped away, Josie's grin became true. "So, what are your plans now?"

"I need to find a place to live."

She frowned. "Why? I heard Bruge fixed up an amazing domit for you."

"He did," Piper said. "I saw it and it's gorgeous. It has three—"

I grunted; the sound filled with disgust. "His mother thinks it's wonderful, too. So wonderful, she moved in." I tentatively touched my cheek where it still stung. "She hit me; would you believe that?"

"Fuck, no," Piper said. "How dare she?"

Rayne's snarl ripped out of her. "Let's find her and show her what happens when you challenge one of us." Her fists clenched at her sides. "All of us will descend on her and show her—"

"Why the hell did she do something like that?" Josie half-shrieked.

"Things were going okay with me and Bruge," I said. "We'd just arrived back and were talking about the domit."

"We're going to want more details about the "while you were away" part, just sayin'," Piper said gruffly. "But keep going."

"His mom came out of the domit, stomped up to me, and announced I smelled like sex." Which… There was nothing wrong with that. "I'm not going to be shamed by that witch."

Ben and Will leaned against my legs, watching us talk.

"Oh, shit, little ears," I said, my face overheating.

"True." Josie gave me a quick, reassuring hug. "No problem. You can catch us up with all that later."

"How do you want us to torture her?" Rayne said,

glaring at a cluster of passing warriors. They took one look at the fury on her face and skittered sideways.

"Slowly," I said with glee, but my cheery façade dropped fast. "Unfortunately, we can't hurt her."

"Why the hell not?" she asked.

"Because she's Bruge's mom. Believe me, I want to teach her a lesson she won't forget, but Bruge said he'd handle it."

Rayne huffed and relaxed her fists. "Say the word, and we're all over her."

Piper nodded. "She won't know what hit her."

"I tell you what," I said. "If she comes at me again, *I'll* be the one swinging first."

"Wanna punch her, Mommy," Will said, his little hands clenched to fists.

Ben held up his own fists and ground his teeth together.

Yeah, that would go over well. The last thing I wanted was for my sons to get into the middle of this. "That's sweet, boys, but I'm going to use my words to fix this, not my fists."

Sure. It was all I could do not to roll my eyes at my own words. But the boys relaxed and leaned against me.

Josie winked at me while Piper and Rayne did all they could not to laugh. "As for where you can live, there happens to be a domit available near mine," she said. "I actually put your things in there to hold it in case someone I knew needed it. I like to pick my neighbors."

"Cool."

She linked her arm through mine. "Let me show you."

The four of us started back down Main Street. "You plan to tell me about the fanged, clawed shaggy horse trailing behind us?"

"Yeah, what's up with the beast?" Piper asked. "If it wasn't staring at you with adoration, I'd be worried."

"That's Fluffy," I said.

"Aptly named," Rayne said. "But where did it come from?"

"She adopted me on our walk back, and I couldn't leave her. Ben named her," I said, squeezing my son's hand.

"She floofy," Ben chimed in. "Thaz why she Fluffy." He dropped back to walk with the droog, clinging to her burnished ruff.

"She sure is, sweetheart," Josie said with a laugh. "So, you and Bruge…?"

Time for a quick change of conversation.

"How goes *your* hunt?" I asked, and she scowled.

"Don't even go there."

"What?" I asked. "That's why we're here."

"Josie's in hate with someone," Rayne said blandly.

"I have no idea why," Piper said. "He's cute. Fun. And I think he likes her."

"He hates me. I hate him."

In hate…? "Who are we talking about?" I asked, looking at all of them. Rayne made the zipper motion with her lips.

Okay, so I'd get it out of her or Piper later. Josie liked someone? Well, she was confident she hated him, but as they say, the two emotions blurred on occasion.

"How long have you been in hate with him?" I asked.

"He's an asshole," Josie said.

"What did he do?"

"He scolded Savvy when she was working with her trundier," Piper said.

"That's not all, but…" She snarled. "Never mind that.

As for Savvy, no one tells my daughter what to do but me. Certainly not some tall, scaly, horned jerk."

"Who's also cute," Rayne chimed in. "Not that I'm looking. Durran is…" The smile she gave me held pure joy. "He's amazing, but I'm not blind. Ze—"

Josie placed her finger over Rayne's lips. "Do not say his name. If you do, he'll appear like your worst nightmare."

Zetar? Just a guess on my part. One of Bruge's warriors, I met him yesterday after I was nearly run over by the narlesks. Interesting.

"Enough about him." Josie grinned. "Did I tell you? Savvy's showing signs she's bonding with Bindy."

"Amazing!" I said. "Bruge said he'd take the boys to the hatchling grounds next season to see if they can form a bond with a trundier, too."

"*You* agreed?" Piper asked, her eyebrows high.

"Sure." I took in the astonishment on my friends' faces. "Jeez. I don't hover over them that much, do I?"

Piper nodded, and a wisp of a smile lifted her lips.

I sighed. "Okay, so I do hover. But only because I'm a careful mom."

"You love your boys," Josie said, giving me a quick hug. "I understand. But since you brought him up, tell me more about Bruge."

"Did you hear?" Rayne said. "He wants to abduct you."

"How did you find out about that?" I shook my head. "He mentioned something about abduction, but what does it mean?" There had to be a joke in here somewhere.

Rayne shrugged. "I think it means he'll abduct you, take you somewhere nice, then have his way with you."

Which…wouldn't be that bad, actually.

Josie leaned in close and whispered. "From what I've heard, seduction comes in after the abducting part."

Did I want something like that with Bruge? My tingling spine shouted yes.

"Where do things stand between you two?" Rayne asked.

"Good question." It seemed I was interested in him from the moment I met him, which was strange as I wasn't the instalove type. Hell, my husband and I dated for two years before we decided to make it permanent.

"That isn't an answer." Josie turned onto a path weaving through short rows of domits.

"But it's all I'm going to say right now," I said.

Josie huffed but good-naturedly. She stopped in front of a domit. "Here's mine." Her arm lifted, pointing to the next in the row. "The free one is right there."

It stood on the outer edge of the village but that wasn't a bad thing. It might be quieter here.

"Let me let Savvy know you're here and then we'll help get you settled," Josie said. "I know where all the supplies are kept."

"Supplies?"

She snorted. "They actually have a domit where they store leaf beds and other assorted furniture they make from plants and creatures around us. You can take whatever you like, though the pickings may be slim now that all the clans have arrived."

I felt like a reject; essentially homeless, and it wasn't a good feeling. Lifting my chin, I reminded myself I had no reason to feel that way. I knew from the start I'd need to claim a new place to live. After a few seasons, I'd get used to the routine and could consider staking out a home we'd use each year.

"I've got to get going," Piper said, giving me a big hug.

"Garek's waiting to take me out for dinner."

I frowned. "How is that possible? Are there restaurants here?"

"He's taking me out, and we're going to have dinner." She wiggled her eyebrows. "He said there's a secluded place on the river where… Well, you understand."

"I do." How wonderful it would be to have someone in my life who wanted to do things like this with me.

"I have to leave with Piper," Rayne said. "Noah's spending the night with me and Missy." She also hugged me, then stepped back. "I'll see you tomorrow? We can work on our baskets together."

"Baskets?"

Her hand flicked out. "Josie will explain."

They left, and I turned to find Savvy bursting from her domit.

"Yay," she said. Tears sparkled in her eyes, and she shook her finger at the boys, who squirmed. "Don't ever do that again, you hear?"

"Nope," Will said.

Ben shook his head adamantly.

"What kind of creature is this?" Savvy said, stooping down and holding her hand out to Fluffy. "Come on, baby! It's time for hugs."

I explained about Fluffy.

"Are there more droogs?" Savvy asked. Her arms wrapped around Fluffy's neck, and she buried her face in the creature's ruff. It seemed the Ferlaern were the only ones who needed winning over.

"I didn't see any others," I said. "You may need to go for a walk and see if you can find one."

"Absolutely not," Josie said. "Our domit is not big enough for a dog the size of a horse. And Savvy's busy enough with her trundier."

"Mom," Savvy sighed, though she grinned at me. "Alien pets are my thing. I want a droog!"

"Think of how nice it'll be to cuddle the dog at night in your furs," I said, hiding my smile from Josie.

"I have blankets for that. Furs, whatever." She turned to her daughter as Savvy stood, still holding onto Fluffy's ruff. The top of the droog's head came to her hip. "I was about to help Alexa settle in the open domit next door. Want to help?"

"Sure," Savvy said. "I'll go grab a few beds and the other things you'll need while you two check it out."

"I'll go with you to help carry things," I said, stepping toward her.

"No need. I won't be carrying them." Savvy lifted her voice. "Anyone want to help an available Earthling woman settle into her domit?"

Five Ferlaern warriors magically appeared, melting out from the main street and other domits.

"Me," Saldarn said.

"No, me." Trudar shouldered his way to the front, flashing his tusks. He dipped forward in a courtly bow. "How are you doing this fine afternoon, Alexa?"

I tried not to snicker at the seven-foot-tall aliens bowing and dipping their heads forward.

Two other males edged forward, nudging Trudar aside.

"I am Udorn," one said, extending his hand.

I shook it but he didn't let go, not until another male elbowed him in the side.

He also took my hand and held it tight. "I am Abesk, and I will do anything to make you happy."

I wasn't sure how to take my sudden popularity.

Their equally adoring gazes fell on me, heavy enough I had to hold myself back from squirming.

"Ben and Will, want to help?" Savvy asked, her gaze

seeking mine for permission to take them with her.

I nodded. She'd watch them like a hawk after what happened. Knowing how upset she was, I wanted to show her I trusted her still.

"Yay," Will said.

Ben jerked his head up and down.

"Awesome." She took their hands then called over her shoulder as she walked away. "Come along, guys. Let's impress Alexa with what we find."

The Ferlaern warriors trooped after her, shooting longing gazes back at us.

"Your daughter's going to be something else when she's twenty," I said softly.

Josie winced. "I'm not letting her date until she's thirty."

My snort rang out between us. "Good luck with that."

Josie sighed and shook her head.

We went inside the domit.

"Because I knew someone might need this unit, I asked a few guys to help weave and encase the frame with new wuldra husk," Josie said as I fingered the material that felt soft yet a tiny bit oily. "At least you won't need to do that. The inner structure lasts between cycles, but the outer must be replaced each year as the old husk dries and falls apart. Wuldra sheds the rain, which I guess we'll see a lot of this winter. I'm sorry. I wish this domit was bigger or that it had separate bedrooms, but the domits were going fast. I imagine the boys can sleep over there." Her hand flicked to the far wall. "And you can place your bed here." She nudged her head to the opposite wall.

About fifteen feet across, it wasn't big, but we wouldn't spend a lot of time here.

"It'll be fine," I said. Cramped, but we'd make do.

"I should've grabbed one of the bigger ones," she said.

"But I thought Bruge…"

"It's okay. Really." I walked to the window and ran my finger across it.

"It's a membranous plant that grows near the river. They stretch it out and tack it to a frame. Voila, a window."

Relatively clear, I could see out. "Well, this place has a water view. I've never had that before." The river churned about fifty feet away and down over a bank. "Do I need flood insurance?" I joked.

She chuckled. "We need to ask because I have the same view."

I dropped down to the floor, leaned against the wall, and stretched out my legs.

Josie joined me.

"How is it here?" I asked. "In general, that is." Since meeting Bruge's mother, I wasn't as excited about settling in the lowlands as I'd been when we left the mountains.

"I really like it. It's louder and more bustling, as there are a ton more people around, but everyone's friendly."

"I assume there's a central dining domit like in the valley?"

"Yes. And we've chosen a big one for our community center. In fact, we're going to host our first event there in two days."

"Already? We just got here."

"It's a chance to gather and meet Ferlaern from the other Clans."

"What's the event?"

"Something you're going to love, my pretty little baker." She smirked. "A silent basket auction."

Ah, so this is where the basket came in. "Refresh my memory. I assume this is part of Piper's new wild west theme?"

"Yup. We've held a square dance, karaoke, though that's really not wild west. And now a silent basket auction. It's a super old dating game thing."

"I assumed. Let me guess. Auction's a given. And I assume we're the prize?"

Her grin widened. "Sorta. We fill a basket with picnic items and the eligible Ferlaern bid on it. Whoever wins spends an evening with the Earth woman on a date, eating the goodies in the basket."

"They don't have money. How will they bid?"

She tapped my arm. "Don't make this complicated. They'll offer skills that will be donated to the central community, and the warlords will dole them out to those most in need."

"And what if we don't want to spend time with the guy who wins our basket?"

"Then you make it a quick, public date."

I sighed. "Will they know whose basket they're bidding on?"

"No."

"And will we know whose bid we choose?"

"Also, no."

"Maybe I want someone to know which is my basket."

Her frown bloomed. "Don't tell Bruge which is yours. That'll take all the fun out of it."

"What about hints?"

She sighed. "Nope, nope, nope."

"I don't know." Did I want to do this? I'd just gotten here and didn't even have a bed to sleep on yet. It seemed silly to spend time coming up with basket items when I still needed to find a domit to set up my bakery, then gather supplies.

"Are you going to do it?" I asked.

She winked. "Sure. It's a chance to get to know

someone who could be the one."

Maybe I already had my "the one". I growled. Unfortunately, Bruge came with baggage in the form of an irritating mother.

"I'll think about it," I said.

"Think fast as you have to sign up by the lunch hour tomorrow."

"All right." So... "I'll do it."

"Just like that?" She grinned.

"As long as they don't mind me bringing the kiddos along on this date."

Piper burst through the door. If she hadn't been grinning, I would've worried my boys were up to something—again. "You need to come with us," she said, holding out her hand. "We've got a surprise."

"I thought Garek had his own surprise for you," I said. "Down at the river."

"Soon." She winked. "Before we leave, we want to do something for you."

I lifted my eyebrows Josie's way. "*We?*"

"Me, too," Rayne said, pushing past the opening. Her hair was askew, and her cheeks were flushed. "While you and Bruge were gone, his friend Zetar—"

Josie's snarl cut off Rayne's words. He was the one. Good guess on my part.

Rayne shook a finger at Josie, her smile not slipping a bit. "Zetar told us about Bruge's plan."

"Oh, the abduction?" I asked.

Rayne's shoulders sagged. "You know?"

Why was she sad about this? "He told me himself. Frankly, I'm not sure what he was talking about. Who abducts women as part of the dating process?"

"The Ferlaern do," Piper said. "It's an ancient—really ancient, that is—Ferlaern tradition. Long ago, the guys would choose a female they liked. If she returned their affection, he'd abduct her and seduce her."

"Seduction sounds like a lot of fun," Rayne said with color infusing her face. From what I'd been able to tell, she and Durran had skipped the abduction and moved right on to the seduction part of this tradition.

"What does that have to do with you two?" I asked.

"Well," Rayne said, her face coloring. "Nothing."

What was she hiding?

Josie studied my face. "Do you want to be abducted and, well, you know, with Bruge?"

I groaned. "Does the entire village know about this?" I mean, seduction was all well and good but if everyone knew what we were doing… My ears had to be scarlet by now. My face sure felt hot.

"Just a few," Piper said, her gaze not meeting mine. Sure. Ugh-ugh-ugh. "Just come with us, okay? Bruge asked us to find you and bring you to the river."

Now? "How long will I be gone? Savvy's coming back with furniture, remember?"

"I'll wait here for them," Josie said with a grin that was too big for the situation.

I frowned. "And the boys—"

"I'll watch them," Rayne said. "Remember? I have Noah already. Two more boys won't make a difference."

You'd think she didn't know my sons.

"I can't leave Will and Ben," I said. They'd miss me. They'd cry for me. They'd—

And there I went again, clinging to them to complete my life instead of doing things solely for me.

"Okay, sure, I could leave the boys for a short while. But why does Bruge want me to join him at the river?"

Piper snickered and took my hand, leading me from the domit. "Don't ask questions. Just come with us."

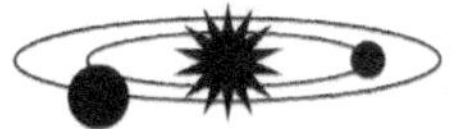

17

Bruge

"You will move into the domit I arranged for you," I told my mother. We stood in the cozy living area I'd furnished for my future mate, something that seemed farther from my reach than ever. "Alexa will move in here with her younglings."

"Is that how you greet your mother?" She strode over to me and turned her face to the side, inviting my kiss.

My lips thinned. "I don't understand why you did this."

She huffed. "I will not leave this domit." Her arms linked on her chest and her tail whipped back and forth behind her, smacking against the coffee table. "You cannot make me."

"I do not need to make you." When would she learn a relationship with Alexa was what I wanted—needed? "If you choose to remain here, I will move Alexa into *my* domit." Never mind that Alexa had already refused.

Mother's composure cracked, and she shifted away from me, putting the sofa between us. "You wouldn't!"

"Why not? She is my mate. She belongs in my bed furs."

"I have someone else in mind for you. She will warm your furs."

"Mother," I said as gently as I could. Despite her behavior, I loved her. I only wished for her to see Alexa as I did. "I do not wish to meet anyone else." I tugged my weapons' strap aside to reveal the symbol. "This shows that Alexa is my maelstrom mate."

Her breath caught. "It's not possible. She is not of our species."

"Yet she is one of many who has formed a maelstrom bond with a Ferlaern warrior."

My mother walked closer, her steps slow due to an old injury to her hip. She'd fallen while training a trundier and walked with a limp since. "Son." Her hand glided down my face. "You know I only want what is best for you."

"That is Alexa."

"She is human. What if she decides to move away or return to Earth? I do not wish to see you hurt."

"She touches something inside me no one else has." I gently took her hand and held it to my chest. "Feel my second heart beating? It does this for her and no one else."

"You cannot love her already."

I shrugged. "Love can come quickly, or it can take a lifetime. I only know that I want to be with her all the time. She makes me happy and when we…"

Her lips twitched upward. "Do not share *that* with your mother."

I pulled her close, hugging her. The top of her head came to my chin, and I rested mine on hers. "Will you try, for me?"

"I do not know if I can, Bruge," she said softly. "Her ways are not ours. She is not one of us."

"We all must try to meet with them in the middle.

Many of us died from the disease but the Earthlings give us hope for a vibrant future."

"I don't like it."

"You do not need to like it, but it would help if you accepted it — if you made an attempt to know Alexa, to see her as I do."

She leaned back in my embrace, and her face remained stoic. "I do not know if this is possible, son."

I bit back my frustration. Being upset with my mother would not make her more eager to reach out to Alexa.

I wanted this female in my life. Could my mother not see that? Setting Alexa aside would rip something apart inside me. But it was the same with my mother. I loved her and wanted her happy, as well.

"I cannot force this, as you know," I said.

"You will truly take her into your domit if I don't relinquish this one?"

"I told you I prepared one for you."

She sniffed, but I could see she was relenting. "I will not apologize to her."

"You assaulted her." Anger burned through me all over again, followed by frustration. This was my mother. I could not treat her as I would a male who caused Alexa harm.

My mother sniffed. "She smelled like sex."

"I am courting her."

She gnashed her tusks. "This is more than courting, my son."

"I plan to abduct her. Seduce her."

She snarled. "How can I convince you she is not the one who will make you happy?"

"There is no way." I linked my arms on my chest and glowered.

"Then she can have this domit." She stormed over to

the sofa and yanked the handmade blanket off the back. "I haven't unpacked yet."

"Thank you." I could force her to apologize, but unless it was given freely, it meant nothing. The best way to win my mother over was to show her how special Alexa was. And her younglings. They could win a possible grandmother's heart.

"I will go to her and tell her I am relinquishing this domit," my mother declared, marching toward the door. "You will not come with me."

I followed, hoping I wouldn't have to snatch her hand from the air.

"Alone," she barked over her shoulder as we left the domit.

"No tricks."

She turned, smiling sweetly. "I would never do anything like that."

I wasn't so certain. "I will ask about your conversation later," I said in warning.

Huffing, she strode down the path.

I remained in front, trying to decide if I should shadow her or collect the other warlords to discuss plans for the season.

Savvy strode past, leading an entourage of males hoisting furniture. Will and Ben walked beside her.

"Bruge!" The younglings barreled into my legs, hugging my knees. I lifted Ben and dropped him on my shoulder. He latched onto my horn and squealed.

"See far," he exclaimed, pointing.

Will leaned into my side and frowned at the other males.

"These items are for Alexa?" I asked Savvy while my mother turned to watch. Brooded, actually. She may be willing to give up this domit, but it would take more than my request for her to relent and treat Alexa as she should.

Savvy stopped on the path and frowned while the males milled around her saying nothing. Udorn and Abesk shot concerned glances at each other, rightly assuming I was competition.

"What's it to you?" Savvy said.

Had she heard about what happened with my mother? She must have.

"Alexa and I will…" I couldn't declare her mine. She had not agreed. I growled as frustration sliced across my hearts. "She will be living in this domit." I swept my hand toward the door.

"That's not what I heard." Savvy shot a raised brow scowl my mother's way. Mother huffed and pivoted, striding away. She held out her hands. "Come on, Ben. Will. We need to go. Your mom is waiting." Her chin lifted and her gaze met mine. "My mother has reserved a domit for Alexa already. A better one."

Saldarn and Trudar shifted furniture from one shoulder to another, watching our conversation with sharp intensity.

"I have instructed my mother to tell Alexa she will have this one," I said.

"What if Alexa wants to live near us?" Savvy asked, her voice softening. "And thanks. Um, actually, the one she's in right now *is* small." She peered around me. "This one has more than one room."

"It has two separate sleeping chambers and a large living space. She and her younglings will be more comfortable here." I rubbed Ben's back, and he jumped up and down.

"Ride pony. Ride pony!" he said.

"He really likes you," Savvy said. "He doesn't go to just anyone, you know."

"They are amazing boys."

Her gaze softened. She cut a glance at the milling warriors before leaning close to me. "For what it's worth, I'm rooting for you."

Roots? Did she mean tubers? No, my translator said… root could also mean cheering for or supporting someone in an endeavor.

I shrugged. "Thank you."

"You better treat her right, though, or I'll come after you." Savvy lifted her fists. Slight, this youngling could not harm even the weakest narlesk, but I would not state this. Everyone clung to a bit of pride.

"Thank you, and you do not need to worry. I am kind," I said.

She snorted.

"Generous."

"That remains to be seen."

Flashing my tusks, I postured. "I am the most appealing male in my Clan."

She rolled her eyes. "Don't push it."

Udorn shuffled his feet, no doubt eager to rush to Alexa and try to claim her. Abesk glared.

Forget it, my friends. She was already taken. I just had to convince her of that fact.

Savvy and I chuckled together, and I was grateful I'd had the chance to speak with her. I wanted the Earthlings to feel welcome here, despite my mother's unsettling greeting. And I wanted Savvy tubering for me. No, *rooting*.

I shifted back and forth, half dancing, to entertain Ben, and he started wiggling along with me. Will looked up at me and grinned.

"I am going to win her basket at the auction," I

declared, feeling stupid the munette I said it because it revealed my intentions to the other males.

Saldarn grunted.

"How did you hear about that?" Savvy asked.

"Zetar told me."

"Oh, him." Savvy's face stilled. "I'm not sure I like him much."

"He is a brave warrior."

"Doesn't mean he's not an asshole on occasion." She slapped her hand over her mouth and gaped at the younglings. "I shouldn't have said that."

"Asshole," Ben said then louder. "Asshole!"

"That's not a nice word, Bennie," Savvy said.

"You say," Will said.

"Yeah, but I'm all grown up," she said. This youngling surprised me whenever I spoke with her.

"I do not see Zetar as a hole in the ass." I liked this term, hole-ass, however. I would use it the next time someone irritated me.

"I'm sure you see a side he hasn't shown me and Mom."

"Perhaps."

"As for the auction, the bidding's going to be tough," Savvy said, frowning as her gaze skipped from Ben to Will. "Seeing as how you're not a…hole in the ass. So far, that is, I could give you a few pointers."

Point… I wanted to smack my translator to make it perform faster. Savvy did not mean a gesture with a poked finger or the tip of a sharp object. Ah, yes, a suggestion. "Thank you."

"I have a feeling you're going to need all the help you can get." She turned to the warriors. "Okay, guys, put everything in this domit instead. No need to truck it all the way across the village only to shlep it back here."

They filed around me and into the domit, each sending me a snarl as he passed. Savvy followed them inside, scooping up Will's hand and taking him with her.

Ben wiggled. "Down."

I lowered him carefully to the ground and he scooted into the domit after his brother and Savvy.

I was about to go after my mother when Zetar jogged over to me.

"Do you have a munette?" He couldn't stop grinning. "Actually, do you have many munettes?"

"For what?" I asked.

"A small thing I have arranged with two of the Earth-ling females."

"What does this entail?" I asked, distracted. My mother was taking her time getting to Alexa. She dropped to her heels at a garden in front of someone's domit and proceeded to start weeding. At this rate, my purple strands of hair would be gray before she did as I asked.

"It entails as much or as little as you would like," Zetar said. He tugged on my arm. "Just come with me, and you will see."

"I'm not sure I have time for—"

A shout rang out at the far end of the village, and a group of Osten warriors galloped to the start of the path on narlesks, then slowed the beasts' pace as they trotted through the village. Dust churned up from their hooves before swirling up into the air.

Odd. I'd expect to see them herding a group of wooly warslettes. The Clan always gathered a sizeable herd after arriving in the lowlands. We penned them and used them for food.

Durran, leading the group, noticed me watching and kicked his beast in the sides, directing it my way. He dismounted when he reached me.

"Unlucky hunting?" I asked pleasantly.

"We have a problem," he said. He swiped his brow while holding onto the reins of his narlesk to keep it from following the others moving toward the holding pen. "We did not find a single warslette herd."

The humor dropped from Zetar's face. I wasn't sure what he'd planned, but it didn't appear I had even a munette to spare to attend to it.

"What do you mean?" I asked. The herds were plentiful, often wandering into the village.

"They are all gone," Durran said. "Tracks show they were herded toward the mountains."

My breath jerked out of me. "You suspect the duskhorde is involved with this?"

Zetar snarled, and his gaze shot to the trundier flock. I expected him to wing into the air within munettes.

Durran raked his fingers through his hair in agitation. "I believe the duskhorde has taken every single one of them."

"I will go after them," Zetar growled. "I will bring them all back."

I held up my hand. "Not yet. We need to meet with the elders and discuss how best to handle this. Durran, can you gather everyone together in the Council domit?"

"I will notify them, but Narcial and Enok opted to travel farther into the plain to look for warslettes. They will not be back until tomorrow."

I bit back my snarl. "Then we will have to wait to discuss this. Could you inform the others?"

"I will." Durran pressed his fist to his chest before spinning and rushing toward the enclosed area to pen up his narlesk.

"I'm sorry, Zetar, but I do not have time for whatever you planned," I said, stepping away from him already. "I need to find Frelz and discuss this." My gaze took in the hundreds of Ferlaern happily preparing their domits. Others worked in their gardens, but it would take too long to grow the crops we savored mid-winter. "If we don't bring back the herds, we will starve."

18

Alexa

"Bruge isn't coming," I said. I crimped my lips together and stared toward the path leading back to the village.

"He'll be here," Piper said, though her enthusiasm was waning. We'd been here at least half an hour.

"I guess we should go back," Piper said.

"Why did you think he wanted to meet me here?"

She watched her foot as she dragged it across the soft soil. "Um…"

"What's going on?"

"Nothing. Let's go back. I'll find…" She shook her head. "Never mind."

Yeah, never mind. It looked like I was stood up.

I liked Bruge, but maybe he wasn't interested in me any longer? I hated thinking this, but after his mother's performance, he might've decided I was too much effort.

Piper and I walked to the village in silence and parted, her going to her domit.

My footsteps dragged as I returned to my own tiny

home. Entering, I sagged against the wall. Then I bumped off and started unpacking my bags.

I didn't get far before someone scratched on the door. Assuming it was Savvy and the warriors with my furniture, I flicked back the flap.

Bruge's mother stood outside.

"You," I said, scowling.

"I could say the same." Her sneer took in my sweaty form before she nudged me aside and entered my domit. "Frankly, I think this residence suits you fine, but my son can be…persuasive."

Had Bruge stuck up for me after all? That warmed me up fast.

"Why are you here, Irella?" I asked, skipping the pleasantries. Frankly, I wanted to curl up on my sofa and get over my most recent rejection.

"I've come to make you an offer."

"No deal," I snapped. "You hit me, and you still owe me an apology before I'll speak civilly with you."

She grunted. "It is wrong to hit another."

I cupped my ear, pushing it forward. "I'm not quite hearing an apology in that statement."

"I respect honesty," she said.

"Still not hearing you."

Her sigh slipped out, and she whispered. "I apologize."

"What was that?"

"I will not repeat it," she snapped.

I swept my hand toward the door. "If that's why you came here, then you can go."

Her shoulders stiffened and she drew herself up, looming over me. "It is not why I am here."

A long silence followed.

"Look, I've got things to do, so get the hell out of Dodge or spit it out," I said in exasperation.

She frowned.

"Tell me why you're here," I clarified.

"I will offer you the other domit on one condition."

"You don't make the rules," I said, stomping toward the door flap. "You don't tell me what to do."

Irella remained where she was, her hands clutching the back of my sofa. Did they tremble? "I also respect a strong person, which I see you are."

"Don't flatter me." I edged closer to her so I could see her face in the dim light. While I didn't trust her, I didn't think she'd strike out again. Not yet. "I'll humor you this one instance. What are your conditions?" As much as it would be nice to live near Josie, this domit was tiny. My boys were boisterous. Okay, they were loud. I'd be yanking out my hair within a sunslice.

"You may have the domit if you promise to stay away from Bruge," Irella said.

Jeez, figures. While my friends and Zetar were trying to get us together, this witch was trying to keep us apart. "This is not your decision."

She stormed closer to me. "You can avoid him. If you do that, he will have time to…meet others."

"Playing matchmaker?" Why wasn't I surprised.

"Any Ferlaern is better suited for him than you."

"I imagine they are, but it's not up to you or them." I stomped back and forth in front of her. "What if I don't want to leave him alone? After all, you said we smelled like sex. Things are progressing well beyond the avoidance stage." Let her bite into that.

"Stay away from my son," she growled, her hands clenching. Here it comes again. Before she could lift her arm, I backed away. If I shrieked, others would come running, though I wasn't afraid of her.

She wouldn't catch me unaware again. I could hold my own in a catfight.

"Bruge is a big boy," I said. "You don't get to decide who he mates with."

"If you avoid him, he will forget about you."

She was wrong. Despite standing me up a few minutes ago, it was clear he liked me. There was no way he'd stay away from me. I shouldn't have to keep reminding myself of that, but here I was. The thought brought a smile to my face. "I'll take the bigger domit, and if it makes you happy, I won't go out of my way to seek him out." I had a feeling he'd be doing the seeking. "However," I said, holding up my hand as she started to gush. "I also won't deny him if he asks me out."

"Asks you…?"

"If he wants to abduct me." No harm in making this plain.

"He will not use ancient traditions with you."

I grinned. "He already has." No need to fill her in on his outstanding offer of abduction. I schooled my expression and tapped my chin. "I have given you my terms. They're good for ten seconds." This tactic worked well with my boys. "Ten. Nine. Eight—"

"All right," she snapped with a nod. "If that is the best we can do."

"It is."

Her tusks ground together. "Then we have a deal."

Perhaps, or perhaps she was about to learn a sharp lesson. "We do."

Someone else scratched on the door.

"Come in," I called.

Bruge poked his head inside and flashed his tusks my way. He looked relieved, as if he expected to see us rolling on the ground, kicking each other. "Everything is settled?"

"If you mean the domit, then yes," I said. "Thank you. I was about to waylay Savvy and direct her to the one you prepared for me."

"I saw her and your younglings already. The warriors are placing your furniture inside it this munette."

"Perfect."

With a soft smile, he held out his hand. I didn't hesitate to take it.

As I passed Irella, I winked.

Chew that, honey, I thought. *Then force it down your twisted throat.*

19

Bruge

I directed my mother to her new domit then escorted Alexa to the one I'd prepared for her.

Fluffy raced ahead of her, rounding the sofa where she jumped up and flopped down onto the cushions with a big sigh.

"It's lovely," Alexa said, running her fingertips across the blanket draped on the back of the sofa. "I, um…"

"What?" I asked, noting her frown. Something was bothering her.

"Nothing. Just…you didn't show up at the river, and I wasn't sure what that meant."

We hadn't arranged to meet at the river, had we?

Will and Ben rushed inside with Savvy. The boys crowded around Alexa, leaping with excitement.

I frowned. "What do you mean about—"

"It's nothing," Alexa said, stooping down to hug Ben. "We can talk about it another time."

Savvy left, and I lingered, watching as Alexa grabbed one of her bags and started unpacking.

The droog watched her move around the domit, her gaze flicking to me.

"I have a meeting in the Elder Council domit tomorrow morning," I said. "Why don't you meet me there by the lunch hora, and we can talk."

"Sure." She shoved hair off her face and gave me a wan smile. "I'll see if Savvy will come hang out with the boys."

What had I missed? I wished I had time to question her to find out. There would be time for Alexa and me tomorrow.

After we come up with a solution to this problem, I would win her basket at auction then abduct her.

20

Alexa

The next morning, my boys and I secured our domit's door flap, telling Fluffy to remain inside. We left the village, walking up the hill I'd taken when I arrived. At the top, I turned to survey the numerous domits. Ferlaern bustled about, and a few trundiers ruffled their wings in the pens on the opposite side of Main Street. But it was early, and most still slept in their beds.

"More walking?" Will sighed. He dropped to the ground and sat with his legs splayed out in front of him.

Ben stood beside me, watching me stare at the village.

"We're not going far," I said. I flicked my hand toward the endless plain covered with stalks, the tops tapping together in the wind. "We're going to play a game and then we'll go to the dining domit for breakfast."

"Game?" Will asked, jumping to his feet.

"Like games," Ben said with a smile.

I held my hand out to him. "Let's see who can collect the most grain from the stalks."

Will tilted his head. "Grain?"

"I'm going to start a bakery, but I need ingredients." By

default, I had a domit I could use for my bakery, the one Josie reserved for me. Unless I could talk the cooks at the dining domit into letting me use their facilities, I'd need to build an oven out back.

"Cookies?" Ben asked hopefully.

"That's ambitious but why not?" I laughed. I didn't have flour or sugar or even one chocolate chip. "We'll need to improvise."

"Like cookies," Ben said.

I herded them from the tramped down area the Ferlaern used as an access road to the village, and out into the tall stalks of grain.

"This is what we need to do." I showed them how to grab the top of the stalk and tug, pulling off the wheat berries. I doubted they were true wheat, but they looked and tasted similar to the grain I remembered from Earth. I'd tried them as we walked back from the trundier adventure. "Put the grains in this." I held up the basket I planned to use for the silent auction in two days. What would I put in it? Something that Bruge would recognize as mine, though I had no idea what.

Moving deeper into the stalks, I continued to strip the berries off the top and deposit them in my basket.

Ben and Will collected a few then proceeded to throw them at each other. A few made it into my basket, so I didn't complain.

I didn't need much, just enough for a few tests.

My basket was half full when I stumbled over something lying on the ground. My heart leaped into my throat, and I caught myself before falling, dumping a third of my grain.

A Ferlaern moaned and rolled onto his back, compressing the stalks.

"What are you doing here?" I asked, recognizing Saldarn. "Don't you have a domit to sleep in?"

He sat up, rubbing his head, and yawned. "I…" He shook, and his black hair threaded through with purple swirled across his back. "I do have a domit, Alexa. A very nice domit." Rising to his feet, he held out his hand. "Would you like to come with me to see it? We can return here later for the younglings."

"I'm not leaving my sons here," I said, irritation sparking through me. I stooped and collected the spilled grain, tossing handfuls into my basket. "As nice as your offer is, I'm not interested in seeing your domit." I straightened and hooked the basket securely over my arm. "Come on Ben, Will," I called out. "I think we've collected enough. It's time to go get breakfast."

Will scowled at Saldarn but said nothing.

Ben skipped over to me and dumped a few more kernels of grain into my basket. He scooted behind me and peeked at Saldarn.

"You will like my domit," Saldarn said. His breath hit my face, sour and in need of mouthwash.

The Ferlaern didn't have anything like toothpaste here, but they used fibrous twigs for brushing. The twigs tasted like coconut, and I'd grown to love the flavor. But since the Ferlaern ate a simple diet, I hadn't encountered stinky breath more than once or twice, and nothing as sour as this. What had Saldarn been into?

I stumbled backward, taking my sons with me. "Thank you, but no. I'm not interested in seeing your domit."

Saldarn growled and stomped after us to the top of the hill and partway down the side. "It won't take long," he insisted. "Once you see what I can offer, you will be interested in mating. You can bring the younglings with you if you'd like." He reached out and ruffled Ben's hair then, before my son could scoot away, he lifted Ben up and onto his shoulder. "Do you like riding? I will be your…puny." He frowned. "Pawnie." With a snarl, he shook his head. "You understand."

Ben's eyes widened and he opened his mouth, releasing a pitiful wail.

Standing beside me, Will joined in.

"Put my son down this instant," I shouted, pointing to the ground. "Do not touch him again."

"He rides," Saldarn said, stumbling around in what he might think was a dance but looked more like a stagger. He patted Ben's back. "You enjoy the ride, do you not, youngling?"

My boys continued to cry.

I chased after Saldarn, jumping up to grab Ben's leg. I didn't want to haul him off Saldarn, but I also refused to allow this male to force my son to do this any longer.

"Give me my son," I bellowed.

"Is there a problem?" someone asked. I turned to see Zetar approaching.

Fluffy bounded after him. She raced past Zetar and up to Saldarn, snarling.

"There is no problem," Saldarn barked. "Not at all." He hastily dropped Ben to the ground and backed away, his hands lifted. "We were playing."

Fluffy stalked him, snapping her teeth.

"Fluffy. Come," I said, tapping my thigh. I scooped Ben up and backed away, taking Will with me.

Fluffy left Saldarn and trotted over to me. She turned and put herself between us, and a fierce growl rumbled in her chest.

"I was making fun with the younglings while courting their mother," Saldarn said, his attention never leaving Fluffy.

"Is that true?" Zetar asked me, scratching his head. "I thought—"

"I don't welcome Saldarn's courtship," I stated plainly, burying my hand in Fluffy's ruff. Will stood on her other side, his hand resting up on her spine. "He forced Ben to do something he didn't like."

"Saldarn," Zetar said with a snarl. "You need to leave Alexa and her younglings alone. She is spoken for already."

"She is not matebonded," Saldarn said, squinting at my arms like he expected to see a maelstrom symbol appear before his eyes.

"I told you I wasn't interested," I shouted.

Fluffy's fur bristled, and if I didn't hold her back, she'd pounce.

"Very well." Saldarn huffed and stalked past Zetar, striding into the village.

Fluffy growled but remained with us.

"Are you all right?" Zetar asked, warily watching the droog.

"Yes," I said. "Thank you." I lowered Ben to the ground, and he clung to my dress.

Fluffy flopped on the dusty soil and rolled onto her back, presenting her belly.

Ben giggled and patted her.

Will watched Saldarn until he'd turned onto a side street and disappeared from view. "Mean man," he whispered.

"Mean," Ben echoed, not looking up from Fluffy.

"I will speak with him, tell him he is not to approach you again," Zetar said, pressing a fist to his chest. "I am sorry."

"It's not your fault. He's a jerk."

Zetar nodded. "He is a hole-ass."

My laughter snorted out. "He sure is."

"Asshole," Will said. "Asshole!"

"No swearing, sweetie," I said, tugging him against my side.

"Asshole," Ben whispered.

Zetar's twinkling eyes sobered. "Tonight, would you be willing to meet me at the trundier pen?"

"Oh, I'm sorry." My face heated. He was nice and all that, but I was only interested in Bruge. Besides, I thought he and Josie…

"Ah, no," Zetar said. "I do not speak for myself."

I frowned. "Then who do you speak for?"

"Oh, um…" Zetar fed me a smile that must make all the Ferlaern females sigh. "You shall see."

Bruge

I skipped breakfast and after speaking with the trundier and narlesk guards, I strode to the Council domit, where I settled on one of the numerous cushions placed in a broad circle. In a circle, no one could claim a higher position. While I hosted here in the lowlands this winter, that task rotated to other warlords each cycle. In the Council domit, we ruled together, with no warlord making demands of the others.

As the other warlords and senior warriors shuffled in and took their own places, I nodded to each.

Once everyone had arrived, Abskin, the appointed elder of the newly formed Cesar Clan lowered the ceremonial stone into the center of the circle, indicating he would run the meeting. "I understand some of you have unsettling news."

Skydar, the Cesar Clan's leader, leaned forward. "I was with Durran and saw this myself. It is horrifying. Not a single warslette could be found."

Skydar was new to leadership but respected by many. In an attempt to solidify warlord status, he challenged

Garek for the powldron that solidified Garek's rule of the Suthen Clan and lost. Skydar initially resented losing his chance to assume control. To add to his distress, Garek formed a matebond with Piper, the Earthling female Skydar hoped to take as his own.

The harm was compounded when Skydar's sister, Meriwee, stole Piper's son. Fortunately, Skydar realized the tragedy his family had created in others' lives. He and his sister left the Suthen clan and came here to begin repairing the domit structures, saving us many sunslices. Once the Suthen Clan arrived, Meriwee apologized to Piper and her son before leaving for the mountains. She would remain there until we migrated for the next season.

They joined the Cesar Clan, and when the leader unexpectedly died, Skydar battled for the role and won.

Another elder, Enok, sipped his tea before lowering the small cup to the floor in front of him. "Please give us all the details. The rumors spreading through the village cannot be true."

"Did you cover enough of the plain?" someone else asked.

"We traveled the usual routes and sent a flight of trundiers farther and…nothing," Durran said.

"I verified this, taking a flight myself and winging farther across the plain," Narcial, the senior Elder of the Suthen Clan said, her frail voice lifting. Highly respected already. "It is horrifying. For generations going back longer than our spoken word, we have come to the lowlands for the winter moons, and we have hunted the warslettes."

"Perhaps we must travel farther afield to locate the herds," Abskin said. "Surely you missed them."

Durran and I shared a heavy glance.

"Do you believe I missed them as well?" Narcial asked wryly.

Abskin's gaze dropped, and he shook his head.

"Did you find any signs indicating where they might have gone, Durran?" Skydar asked. He'd changed over the summer moons; he'd matured into a decent leader—a position one had to fight to hold onto. There were no powldrons for him to claim, so he would never achieve full warlord status, but he appeared to be satisfied for now with his current role.

"On our way here from the mountain valley, we spied a large tribe of duskhorde crossing the plain," Durran said.

"This is not new," Skydar said. "It is common to see them in this region." He frowned. "I saw considerable duskhorde movement before the rest of you arrived, and a lot of movement toward the north."

"Dusklen with warslettes?" I asked.

"Only small herds," Skydar said.

"As he arrived in the lowlands, Zetar saw dusklen driving herds into the mountain valleys and beyond," I said. "He followed until they reached the bigger clans beyond the great passage."

The great passage sliced through the top of the broad, most northern mountain range, and was the only access to the enormous plains beyond.

"Why would they make such effort to move warslettes?" Garek asked, and I was pleased to note Skydar listened politely. "Do they not have creatures they can hunt on their own plains?"

"It makes no sense," Zetar said. "Perhaps they are not finding enough to eat this cycle?"

"I do not believe this is why they do it," Durran said, his solemn gaze meeting mine. He'd recently bonded with his uncle's powldron, solidifying his claim to the Willen Clan.

"You believe they do this to starve us," I said.

He nodded. "Why else take them? They left us nothing."

Zetar growled. "I will go after them. I will bring back the herds."

"I suggest we send a group of warriors," I said, flashing my friends a grim smile. "The duskhorde are not the only ones who can sneak onto a plain and steal stock."

"What will keep them from following and taking them again?" Skydar asked.

"We will have to guard the herds." A nearly impossible task, however.

I felt more than uneasy about this. We'd never had friendly relations with the duskhorde. How could we when they'd be happy to eat us, given the chance? But we had never taken our feud to this level before.

"That will not be simple," Narcial said. "The warslette are not creatures who can be placed in a pen like the narlesk. They range freely. It is their way."

"I cannot think of another solution," I said. "Can anyone else?"

We all stared at each other in dismay.

"We will think on this," Narcial said. "And we will find a solution." She turned to Zetar. "What else did you see when you followed them? Perhaps a solution can be found if we have more information."

He nodded slowly but by the creases on his face, I could tell he wasn't convinced. "I followed them until they met up with a larger tribe on the upper plain. They passed our domits in the valleys but did not stop."

"The remaining trundiers are safe?" Skydar asked. "The horde did not attack them?"

"The hatchlings have grown large enough to travel. They came here with us," Durran said. Before he bonded with his powldron and took over the Willen Clan, he served as a head trundier trainer. "The only trundiers left behind were those who have never formed bonds with a Ferlaern."

"They are nearly feral," I said, remembering an encounter with one that nearly bit my head off when I came too close to its nest.

"The horde ignored them as they passed," Zetar said. "Odd for a group of people who are so hungry they would steal all the warslettes from the plain."

"We must assume this is not motivated by hunger," Abskin said. "They hope to starve us."

"A very real possibility if we cannot find warslette." I turned to Zetar. "We need to fly farther afield, seeking herds. Perhaps they did not capture them all."

"Yes," Narcial said. "This is good. If we can locate other herds, we can watch them, only taking what we need to survive."

We hunted selectively, bringing down only the weakest and leaving the strong to reproduce for another cycle.

"This does not address the duskhorde, however," Skydar said, his voice strained. "We cannot let this insult go unchallenged."

"Our needs must come first," Garek said, and Skydar reluctantly nodded. "Yes, we should seek farther for herds, but how can we address this issue in another way? Piper has spoken of Earth, how some species have become extinct over time. We have become too dependent on the warslette. Perhaps it is time to think of other sources of food?"

"What else is there to eat?" Skydar asked. "It has always been the warslettes."

"In the past, when the herd was too thin or sick, we ate narlesks," I said. "Yet I don't like thinning that herd. It will take time to find other herds or steal some back from the duskhorde and drive them back to the plain."

Abskin grunted. "A sickness passed through this past summer, killing many of the narlesk young. While we could cull a few of the older, weaker beasts, I'd prefer to maintain our herd at its current size for this cycle."

A sound at the door made a few of us turn, but there was no one there. The wind rustling the flap?

"We are nearly four hundred people," Garek said. "The supplies we brought with us will not get us through this cycle."

"With the Earthlings here, our numbers are greater," my mother said with disgust. She was not a warlord or an elder, but she maintained an honorary position on the Council as my father's widow. She'd advised him wisely, and I welcomed her input in this situation, though I did not like how she attacked the Earthlings at every turn. "They take too much."

"There are only twenty adult females," I grumbled. "They are small in stature. They eat little."

"They bring us a future," Durran said, shooting my mother a sharp look. "And you complain that they must also eat?" His snort of disgust made my mother slump low on her cushion. "You forget the younglings they brought with them." His chin lifted, and his steely gaze met hers, which dropped. "My Rayne quickens already with our own child."

Garek slapped Durran's shoulder. "Congratulations. When do you expect your youngling to arrive? Piper will deliver partway through the next summer in the valley."

Two females pregnant with younglings bridging our two worlds. I marveled at the wonder, and my mind took me down a road I might never travel. Me and Alexa. Her younglings being raised by both of us.

My mother watched me and there was no missing her frown. She guessed what I thought and did not like it.

"No matter how many we are, we still need to eat," she said, relenting. "We can collect tubers and fish in the river, but that will not be enough."

My belly carved out, but I didn't fear hunger. I more worried about keeping the younglings and pregnant females from starving.

Another sound at the door made me turn.

"What about the grain?" Alexa asked, stepping inside the domit. As she strode toward us, her nervous glance took in the stern elders and puzzled warriors.

I welcomed her input. As Garek said, Earthlings had seen extinction on their own planet. How had they adapted?

"You were not invited to this meeting," my mother said, starting to rise.

I held her back with a hand on her arm.

"What do you mean?" I asked Alexa, urging her forward with a flash of my tusks.

"Back on Earth, I was a baker. When we lived in the mountain valley, I experimented with various grains I collected there, and I've discovered those growing in this region are related."

"A few handfuls of grain will not feed hundreds of Ferlaern," Mother said, turning away from Alexa, dismissing her.

"You're right," Alexa said. She dropped down to the floor beside me and grinned up at me before turning a raised brow look at my mother. "Which is why I don't suggest something that simple. I brought designs for wood-fired ovens, and I'm confident we can build them on the upper plain. The grain growing around us will work with my recipes." She stiffened her shoulders when she noted the others staring at her with shock.

Were they stunned by what she said or that she felt confident enough to walk into a Council meeting and propose something astounding?

"I'll need help," she added weakly. "Collecting enough for all of us will take time, and grinding will be a lot of work as I only brought a few hand mills. And then I'll need others to help make the bread. I realize what I offer won't be enough to feed everyone, but if we supplement it with tubers and fish and whatever else we can gather on the plain, it could make a difference."

My mother's mouth dropped, and she sent me a look I couldn't define.

If I didn't know better, I'd say she was starting to feel a bit of respect.

22

Alexa

"I actually didn't come here to interrupt your meeting," I said. "But I think I can contribute something that'll help us all." I held up the plans for a simple oven we could build and feed with wood. "We'll need to build four, I think, to keep up with demand."

Bruge took them and looked them over. "This isn't like anything I've seen before." His gaze met mine, and the confidence I read there gave me the boost I needed in this room full of serious Ferlaern.

"From what I can tell, bread is unheard of here," I said. "Back in the valley, I cultured a sourdough starter. It was my grandmother's recipe and it's the simplest leavening agent. Yeast can be derived from the air around us, but we have no way of knowing how the finished product will taste. Actually, some Belgian beers are fermented this way; they opened the windows and let the natural yeast in the air turn the wort into beer. But I didn't want to experiment with unknown yeast."

An older elder shifted, frowning, and Bruge's mother

wore the expression she took on whenever I was around, a frown.

Bruge nodded slowly, but I could tell I'd need to win more than him over to my idea. I surged on, desperate to convince the others I could help. "There's enough grain to see us through the season. And bread is the perfect staple in anyone's diet."

"You are sure the grains growing around us can be turned into food?" Narcial asked. I couldn't tell if she was skeptical or supportive, as her lined face gave nothing away.

"I'm surprised you're not gathering them already to make something similar to pemmican," I said. "Long ago on Earth, indigenous people combined pounded meat with melted fat, dried berries, and grains, creating a portable meal that was much like a protein bar."

"We have made such a thing in the past," Narcial said, nodding slowly.

"I cannot see how this will help," Bruge's mother said, shifting uneasily on her cushion. "You need to leave and let us continue our discussion."

"Allow her to finish," Narcial said, not sparing Irella a glance.

"If we can collect grain and remove the outer husk, then grind it in my hand mills." I had to be the only person to bring hand mills from Earth, but I had a feeling they'd be needed. "We can turn the grain into flour. While some are gathering and preparing the grain, others can help me build ovens to cook the bread I'll prepare from the flour."

"How long will this take?" Narcial asked.

"A few weeks for the collected grain to dry. We'll need a lot, but the plain is covered with it. I saw this while Bruge and I walked back after collecting my sons. While the grain is drying in domits, we'll build the ovens. As I said, four should be enough."

"I like this idea," Narcial said. Her gaze swept across the others before pinning Irella in place. "Do any of you have a better suggestion?"

Irella's gaze dropped. Despite my urge to fist pump the air, I held still, keeping my face neutral. Even Irella needed to hold onto her pride.

"I agree," Bruge said, flashing his fangs my way again.

My spine flamed. If only we were alone. I still didn't know why he hadn't shown up last evening, but my humming body said it was okay if a meet-up slipped his mind.

"I am putting my full trust in you, as will the other warlords," he said, his smoldering gaze trailing down my body.

Flames? Meet fire.

I suppressed the feeling. This was not the right place. We'd have to find time soon, however.

"I, for one, am interested in tasting this brood," Narcial said grandly. "Do you have samples?"

"I brought flour I hand ground in the mountain valley. I'll make you something you can try."

Narcial dipped her head forward, and when her eyes met Bruge's, she nodded. Was this her way of showing she approved of *us*? Silly of me to think our relationship came into this.

Irella would be harder to convince. For one tiny moment, I actually wanted to try.

No, I wanted Bruge in my life. If I could only have him with her trotting along behind him, I'd take it.

My heart flipped. I'd prove this idea could work, not just to him and Narcial, but to his witch of a mother.

Okay, I might need to stop calling her "witch".

I didn't need her to like me, but it would be nice if she showed me some respect.

"I'll need help doing this. I can't do it alone," I said, and the elders grunted.

"I will assign a team of warriors," Bruge said. "Some will gather grain while others build these…oovens."

"I have warriors who will help as well," Garek said eagerly.

Durran and… Skydar, I think his name was, also offered males to help.

The grain growing in the mountains tasted like rye, and a recent taste of the local fare told me this was similar, though its flavor more closely resembled wheat. My belly rumbled at the idea of bread baking in an oven.

"We can eat bread with our meals." I frowned. "I should mention that I overheard some of your earlier conversation." Enough to know we were in big trouble. Damn duskhorde. Why wouldn't they leave us alone? "Can we set traps to capture other edible creatures?"

"Yes, and there are smaller beasts we can hunt," Durran offered. He dipped his head my way, showing approval.

I beamed inside but wisely kept my face solemn as Irella continued to squirm at the attention paid to me.

"We need to take care not to deplete the fish stock in the river," she said.

"So, bread, tubers, fish, the creature you mentioned, plus…" I said. "What else can we eat? With flour, I can make other baked items, but one thing at a time." Piper was going to get her pancakes one day. "I'll start with a simple sourdough bread or even an unleavened bread that can serve like pita or naan." My belly jumped again, eager already. There was nothing I missed more than a slice of hot, crusty bread coated with butter. And a cookie! I'd almost die to bite into one now.

"We milk the narlesks," Abskin said. "That can be consumed as well."

"If I can have some milk, I can use that, too," I said. "I assume the birds I see flying around lay eggs. Are there any that nest on the ground and only fly a limited distance?" I thought of turkeys and chickens, the Ferlaern version of them, that is. "If we capture and pen them, we can collect their eggs. They're tasty as well."

"I think I know a creature that will fit," Bruge said. "When I was a youngling, I used to creep close to the slidarns and steal their eggs. My mother would cook them. I will ask warriors to build pens and then to capture as many as possible."

"We'll need to feed them, and we are wrong to assume this will be simple," Irella said. As always, she was eager to knock my ideas down. She wasn't going to make this easy for me, but I was worthy of the challenge.

The local version of a fly buzzed near my face, and I swatted it away. Pesky things were everywhere. "If the slidarns eat something like this, we're in business." Excitement took hold of me, making my pulse sing. "Soon, we'll have more food than we can imagine."

"You are amazing," Bruge said, shaking his head. His long, black hair shot with purple swayed on his back, and when he flashed his tusks, I was reminded of how attractive I found him.

"Very well, then," Narcial said. "Let us adjourn the meeting." Her attention fell on me. "Are you available later to help formulate a full plan?"

When Irella huffed, I held in my grin. "Of course."

"Then let us leave to discuss this with our warriors," Skydar said. "I will send them to you early tomorrow?"

"Thank you," I said.

Everyone left but Bruge.

I lingered, even when his mother shot a dark look my way.

Once the door flap glided closed, leaving us alone inside the building, Bruge's smile widened. He rose and tugged me up from the floor, his arms wrapping around me.

"Thank you," he whispered. "You have saved the Clans."

"I haven't done anything yet," I said, the weight of responsibility heavy on my shoulders. "But I'm going to try."

"That is all any of us can do."

My body heated up at the close contact, and I wondered if we could sneak off to be alone together.

He flashed a smile my way. Then he took my hand and guided me through the village to a domit a few away from mine, stopping outside where he cupped my face.

"I want you," he said.

"Yes," I breathed, my body tingling.

We went inside, and he led me to a huge bed off the main living area.

"Alexa?" he asked. "Where are the younglings?"

"With Piper," I said, my voice thready. "I told her I'd pick them up soon." Solid lust swirled through me. I wanted him. Wanted *this*.

"Then I will give you a taste of our future." He lifted me and his mouth devoured mine. It was fast and furious, and I wouldn't have it any other way.

Dropping down onto the bed, he tugged my dress up, his rough fingers gliding across my skin.

He parted my thighs and crawled between them. "You smell fantastic. Sweet and juicy."

"Juicy is not a word anyone should use with sex," I gasped out as his fingers teased my clit.

"No?" he murmured. His long, scratchy tongue glided across my opening.

My mind exploded. "Um, err, no."

"Are there any other forbidden words?" He sucked my clit into his mouth, and I shrieked.

Fuck… What was he asking? Oh, yeah, forbidden words. "Moist. We don't use that one either to describe our pussies."

He lifted his head. "Pussy? What is this pussy?"

I latched onto his horns and guided him back to my body. "Never mind. Just… Just…"

His tail flicked around and latched onto my clit. Another shriek burst from me.

He chuckled and glided one of his thick fingers inside me. "You are responsive, mate. I adore this. I adore you."

I widened my legs, and he licked from the bottom to the top then dipped his tongue inside me, joining his pumping fingers.

"Shit, shit," I said.

"None of that. Allow me to savor the moist juiciness of your pussy."

Ugh. How could he make those words sound sexy?

His fingers pushed harder. Thicker. No, wait, it was his tail.

My body burst into an inferno.

The tip of his tail stroked my G-spot, and my hips jutted upward before I could contemplate saying anything.

"Bruge," I moaned, coming undone. His tail felt so good. Who the hell would've thought this part of his body could…? My mind spiraled away as I gave into the overwhelming pleasure.

As he pumped into me, hitting deep inside, his tongue flicked across my clit.

"I can't hold out," I cried.

"Don't, Alexa. Come. Explode for me so I can feel it. I need it."

"Bruge!" I coiled tight. Everything inside me was about to fling itself into outer space. "Don't stop." I lived for each movement inside me. For his tongue on my clit. His fingers teasing my folds.

For this male who only wanted to give me pleasure.

"What about you?" I somehow found the brains to gasp out.

"I will claim you completely, but not now. We do not have time. But soon. Then I will pleasure you all night."

A night of wild, hot sex with Bruge sounded like the most appealing thing in the world. I wanted it. Gritty. Hard. And overwhelming.

His tail went faster, and I hitched my legs up onto his shoulders, coiling them around to hold him tight.

When he gently bit down on my clit with his tusks, I fell apart, flung up into the sky.

I cried out his name.

He soothed and stroked me until I flopped back onto the bed. Then he lifted his head and grinned.

23

Bruge

I wanted to taste her again, but she needed to collect her younglings from Piper, and there was no time. My mate was sweet and infinitely satisfying. I could not wait to claim her fully.

After helping her dress, we left my domit and strolled to Piper's, where I left her at the door flap.

I located warriors for each project and gave them their assignments. They might be skeptical, but soon they would see. My mate was clever, and the clans would herald her as our master of food.

With my warriors assigned duties, I went to my trundier and ensured he was happy and well-fed. He nudged my chest hard, making me stumble a few steps backward. "Would you like to take Alexa and I for a trip?" I whispered.

Nykas huffed as if he understood. Perhaps he did. Trundiers were smart, almost as smart as my glorious mate.

The culier threads on my cock ached. They wished to be buried inside her, to stroke her inner walls and the intriguing bump my tail discovered inside her. When I touched it, her hips jerked forward, and her cries grew more feverish. I wanted to explore that nub until I elicited the same response again.

Grinning, I left Nykas, bumping into Zetar who growled, though more in frustration than anger.

"What bothers you, friend?" I asked, unable to imagine what could bring about that sound.

"*Her.*"

"Ah. Female troubles?" It was easy to mock when I felt confident about Alexa. I had not shown her my matebond symbol or asked her to be my mate, but I would soon.

Zetar must be in the early throes of courtship. I held in my smile, as my friend would not appreciate the gesture.

As we walked together back toward the village, I looped my arm over his shoulders. "Tell me about this female trouble."

He shrugged me away, his lips thinning. "This… This… She makes my brain burst into a thousand pieces."

"Who is the female who does this to you?" It must be one of the Earthlings.

"I do not wish to say."

"You do not want to…janx it?" Janx was a word I learned from the Earthlings. I liked the sound of it and its meaning. At Zetar's frown, I explained.

He nodded. "Yes, I do not wish to…janx this."

"Very well. But if you wish for assistance in your courtship, you know the way to my domit."

"I do not know if I wish to court her or push her away."

"Yet, here you are, fuming about her."

He reeled away from me; his face heavy with creases. "Again, I have no idea what to do with this impudent female."

"I see." I bit back my smile. Hate and affection were close friends. I would watch to see how this progressed. "Is there anything I can do to help?"

His head dipped forward, and he growled out a sigh. "I give thanks, but I will handle her myself. She just…" Snarling, he stiffened his spine. "I will show her who is the warrior and who is the maiden."

Oh, he would, would he? If she was anything like my Alexa, he was in for a wild ride. I hoped whoever he was fuming about showed him the joy of a maelstrom bond. My friend deserved that after the rough upbringing he had.

He started to stride away from me but turned back. I swore I read mischief in his eyes but why would I?

"Actually, you could help me as the sun slakes across the horizon," he said.

"What do you need?" I asked with some hesitation.

"Can you meet me at the narlesk pens?"

"Of course."

"Bring…" He chuckled. "Actually, you do not need to bring anything but yourself."

Something was going on here, but I couldn't quite place why I felt uncertain. "All right."

"Good." He slapped my shoulder, an Earthling gesture many of us had adopted. "I will see you then."

After he left me, I walked to Rayne's domit to ask her the rules of the upcoming basket auction. It was vital I beat out my competition. Many would wish to spend time with Alexa, and I had plans for the next sunslice that did not include any of my warriors.

Abduction and seduction were still in the forefront of my mind.

When I did not find Rayne in her domit, and Durran wasn't around—I assumed they were together—I walked across the village, wondering who I could ask advice from instead.

Along the way, I stopped and spoke with five of my warriors, discussing the domits we would use to pen the slidarns. The door flaps would need to be secured, and I wanted pens constructed on the backs that would allow the creatures to roam free, though contained. And we needed to protect them from predators.

After leaving them with the task, I crossed the village, studying our fortifications. We built out in the open on purpose so we could see predators coming. I made mental notes for ways we could add security. I'd speak with my warriors this evening after I dealt with Zetar's task.

As I was returning to my domit, I found Narcial puttering in the wide garden alongside her domit.

When we lived in the mountains, Durran once told me Narcial gave him excellent advice that helped him win Rayne. Perhaps she could help me, as well.

"Do you have time to talk with me?" I asked her.

Rising to her feet, she gripped my forearms and flashed her tusks. "Always, Warlord Viskariast. What would you like to speak of?"

A few warriors stood nearby, grousing with each other, but their voices stilled at Narcial's words, and I swore they cocked their heads to listen. One snickered — of that I was sure.

"Not here," I said, struggling not to squirm under the weight of their glances.

A sly frown filled her face. "I see."

"What do you see?" Sometimes, I swore everyone in my Clan saw things but me.

Tipping her head back, she cackled. "I know who you wish to speak of."

"I have not said I needed to speak about anyone in

particular." I tried to sound affronted, but how could I? I wanted her help. "Let us walk along the river. We can talk confidentially there."

Leaving my chuckling warriors, Narcial and I took the path to the river then walked along the bank.

Periodically, Narcial stopped to dig random tubers, placing them in her sack, and I did the same until the bag bulged. Our clan would need to allot additional time for hunting and gathering. We'd become lazy with an endless supply of warslettes.

"What do you wish to speak of?" she asked, stopping to stare across the broad river. It slowed in this section, and through the gleaming surface, I caught movement. Large fish plied these waters, and one would feed a clan for a sunslice with only a few fish. We were many, but so were they.

With Alexa's baking, I began to find hope we would find a way to get through this cycle with full bellies.

"I need your advice about an Earthling game," I said. "One where males win females as the prize."

"Which game is this?" she said with a snort. "There are so many."

"One that uses baskets."

"Ah, I know of what you speak," she said.

"You do?"

"Naturally." Her tusks flashed my way. "I have done the hanging with Piper and Rayne."

My translator suggested something unpleasant involving rope. "Hanging...?"

"Yes, I have done the hanging where we sit and chat, much like you and I do now. We hang." She stooped down and carefully peeled a brigard off a plant. She offered it to me but when I shook my head, popped it into her mouth, her teeth churning. After swallowing, she spit out the center seed.

Alexa used a similar term. It was… "Hanging out together." This sounded much more pleasant.

"Yes, hanging." She nodded pertly. "As for the basket auction, your bid needn't be the highest to win the maiden you wish to claim."

"Then how does one win?"

"The female will choose the offer she likes best. That is the rule."

"How do I ensure my service is the one that will have the most appeal?" And how did I ensure Alexa picked me?

"What you truly must be asking is, does this female wish for you to win her basket?"

"I see." Alexa would find my offer the most appealing, would she not? "I wish to abduct her."

"And seduce her." Narcial nodded slowly. She peeled off another brigard and ate it. "So is our way. I approve, youngling."

She knew I was not a youngling. "You tease me."

A tug on my hair was followed by her grin. "And you enjoy this."

My mother never did anything like this. As the mate of our Clan's warlord, she approached life with a serious demeanor that never faltered.

"If she had smiled or laughed every now and then, she would be a happier female now," Narcial said softly. "And you a happier male."

"How do you know what I think?"

"It is written in the lines on your face."

"My skin is segmented. This is why I have lines on my face."

"We speak of your mother who rarely laughed or found munettes of joy. It is a shame."

Stopping, I dug another tuber and added it to the bag I now carried for her.

"I can see all," Narcial said.

I scoffed. "No one sees anything but what is in front of them."

Stopping on the path, she turned, her brow scrunching. "I do not believe my gift is what the Earthlings call… mageek? I do not remember the exact word. No, I have only lived long enough to understand how Ferlaern think and behave."

"Not Earthlings."

"They are not so different from us, as you have come to see for yourself."

Alexa's cries of pleasure echoed in my mind, and I grinned.

"You have begun the seduction part of this already." She tapped my arm. "In your haste to claim her, do not forget the most important part of the tradition, abduction."

"I will not," I vowed with a clenched fist to my chest.

"If you do not make haste, others will…help you with this."

My mind shot to Zetar's odd request to meet him at the trundier pen this evening. My friends—the village—wouldn't… No. They would not try to handle this for me. It was the task of the warrior doing the courting. "What are you speaking of?" I tried to read the… all right, lines in her face, but she gave nothing away.

She cackled.

"Narcial," I said firmly.

She patted my arm. "It is nothing. Come."

We continued walking, her humming, me pondering Zetar's request.

"Do you believe Alexa will see the worth of my offer and choose me?" I asked, getting back to the auction.

"Perhaps and perhaps not."

I tried to huff but it came out a growl. "I should not be jealous if she chooses another."

"She wants only you, but you must play these Earthling games to win her. Then you can fully claim her as your maelstrom mate."

"You knew I possess the symbol?" Few did, as my weapons' straps covered the mark on my shoulder.

"I did not see it, but I think…" Her head tilted and she paused, her face filled with strain as she sought inward. "I can sense your second heart beating. And I see how you watch her. Adoration gleams in your eyes."

I wore the feeling with pride. Some males might puff and scoff at emotions, but not me. If Alexa wanted to be with me, I would cry out my happiness to the world.

"Win the basket and abduct her. I," she tapped her breastbone, "will stay with her younglings. I promise they will be safe while you are gone."

"They are a challenge, one almost as great as Alexa."

"One I feel worthy of taking on. You forget, I raised five younglings myself."

I *had* forgotten. "Will and Ben are three-cycles-old."

"I need youth around me to keep me young," she said, smacking her tusks together. "I will teach them new skills. Perhaps one will grow up and choose to become an elder."

That would be a sight to see: an Earthling wise one advising our Clans. I hoped I lived to see this day.

"We must return," she said, staring toward the village in the distance. The sun would sink below the horizon soon and I needed to meet Zetar at the narlesk pens.

We turned on the path and strode back toward the village.

"I sense unease coming to our land," Narcial said. "We must prepare."

"How does one do this?" I asked, feeling overwhelmed. There was so much to do and so many chances to miss one detail that could make a difference.

"First, we will do what your maelstrom mate needs so she can prepare this brood for our meals. Then, we will fortify our village."

"You believe the duskhorde will attack?"

"Is that not their way?"

"They have migrated beyond the great passage," I said. "Perhaps now that they have stolen all the warslette, they will never return."

Her penetrating gaze met mine. "Do you believe they will never return?"

I sighed. "No. They will not stop until they have consumed us all in one way or another."

"So, a fortress."

"You suggest a wall?" I couldn't imagine living behind a barrier. The Ferlaern were meant to roam free.

"Not a wall, but we can turn ourselves into this fortress with cunning. We will think and find a way."

"When do you believe the duskhorde will return to the plain?" I asked.

Her rheumy gaze scanned the horizon bleeding blood red. "Too soon."

Alexa

When it was time to meet up with Zetar, I couldn't go. When I saw him in the morning, I'd apologize and set something up for another time. Surely whatever he'd planned could wait.

Ben hurled into the bucket, his tiny body shaking.

"It's okay," I said, smoothing his hair away from his face. Fortunately, he was only vomiting up bilious liquid. "Did you eat anything else other than dinner?" I'd picked out his food myself. My poor youngest son had an unsettled stomach, and it didn't take much to set him off. Once he started throwing up, it didn't stop until he'd slept.

"No," he moaned, his belly rumbling. He clutched the sides of the bucket and shuddered.

Will stood on his other side, his face creased with concern. He patted Ben's back, like me.

"Okay, Bennie?" he asked again.

"Done," Ben said, prying his fingers off the bucket's sides.

I lifted him up and carried him to his bed then laid

down with him, holding him in my arms. "It's gonna be okay, little guy."

"Yucky, Mommy," he said. "Hate yucky."

Smoothing his hair to the side, I kissed his forehead. His eyelids drooped already as his body welcomed sleep.

"Rest, sweetie. You'll feel better in the morning."

Will joined us on Ben's other side, his arm going around his brother's waist, and Fluffly flopped onto the floor beyond Will.

Ben fell asleep. Will did, too. Fluffy watched but kept stifling a yawn.

Next thing I knew, sunlight stabbed my eyelids.

And someone was scratching on the door.

I eased away from Ben and rose, smoothing my hair as I hurried to the door. When I tugged the flap aside, I gulped.

Ten burly warriors stood on the path outside, shifting their feet.

"We have come to work on the oovens," Frelz said, dipping his head forward. "Yesterday, we collected rocks as Bruge directed. We have piled many on the plain above the village."

"Oh, okay, sure. Come on in," I said.

Good thing our domits were tall because these guys were enormous. And when ten of them stuffed themselves inside my generous living area, I was tempted to sell tickets to this alien muscle man show.

Frelz bowed again. "We are here to begin construction on the ooven to cream grain into a substance you will use to construct food." His face creased with confusion and frankly, I felt the same.

The others watched him, universally unblinking.

"We're going to grind the grain and we'll use the flour to make bread we'll bake in the wood-fired ovens," I said.

"I know you haven't had bread before, but you're going to love it."

The other guys loosened, milling around looking skeptical until my boys heard the commotion and woke up.

I was never more grateful to see normal color in Ben's face.

Will jumped up and ran around the sofa, skidding to a halt, his arms outstretched.

Ben bumped into his back.

"Whoa. Lotsa big guys." Will tilted his head. "Mommy, why all big guys here?"

"Big," Ben said, his eyes enormous. "Berry big."

"They sure are, sweetie," I said, striding around the guys to pick Ben up. I placed him on my hip, and he yawned and leaned his head on my shoulder. "I want to go with you to lay things out per my drawing," I told Frelz. "But I need to find someone to stay with the boys first."

"I will remain here with the younglings," someone said from behind the guys. Narcial, the senior elder wove between them, a slender doe among a herd of towering, golden moose. She flashed her tusks at me. "It has been too long since I spent time with children."

I…wasn't sure. I mean, I completely trusted Narcial. She was a sweetie, and she'd never allow a bit of harm near my boys. But maybe they should go with me.

"I see what you think," Narcial said, her smile holding true. "And you needn't worry. They will be happy here with me." She held out her hands. "Come, younglings. I believe it is time you were educated in the history of your illustrious Clan."

"Which Clan?" I asked because we'd lived with the Suthen all summer and now, for the winter moons, we mingled with them all.

"The Nulet Clan, of course. Bruge's Clan."

The warriors watched our exchange more intently than guys at the latest action movie.

"I'm not part of Bruge's Clan," I said.

One of Narcial's thick brow ridges lifted. "Are you not?" She came toward me, humming, then strode around me, checking me out. Her cackle rang out. "I say you are, or you will be soon."

What the hell did that mean?

The guys shuffled their feet and a few looked poised to flee. I couldn't have that, as I needed their help.

"Okay," I said. "It would be wonderful if you'd stay here with Ben and Will. Ben was sick last night but he seems to be feeling better now. Go lightly with the food and beverages, however, or he'll start vomiting again."

Narcial frowned. "I see. We will eat—carefully—and then return here," she said. "Will that suit?"

"Okay, sure." I gnawed on my lower lip while unease skittered down my spine.

Why was I stressing about my boys? Probably because, every time I left them, they got into trouble.

"You'll watch them like a hawk," I said. The moment I realized I clung to Ben, I lowered him to his feet. He leaned into my side, watching the "berry" big guys.

"I do not know this hark, but of course I will take care," Narcial said benignly. "I have a way with younglings. You will see."

Watching Will edge toward the door made me doubt how sophisticated her "ways" were, but she was an elder.

What trouble could they get into while I wasn't around?

Lots.

However, I promised myself I'd stop hovering over them all the time, that I'd give them the chance to make simple mistakes and learn from them. I doubted anything would happen with Narcial around.

"I won't be gone long. Maybe twenty minutes." I'd hurry this as much as I could. I flicked my hands out toward Frelz and the guys, smiling at Bruge's friend, Zetar as he joined the group. "Ready to go?"

Zetar grinned. "Yes, we are ready."

"Building ovens is hard work," I said. "We'll need to harness all your power."

He frowned and lifting an arm, flexed an impressive muscle. "This is power."

He rivaled Bruge for hotness, and I wondered if he was single or not. I'd worm it out of him while we talked about how to build the mill. Maybe I could fix him up with one of the other Earthlings.

Josie, for example, since she was still on a hate fest with her mystery male.

"You do have impressive muscles," I noted. "We'll enlist that power in a few weeks to grind the grain."

"This, I will enjoy seeing," Zetar said with a flash of his tusks.

"Stay with Narcial, Will, Ben," I said, as Ben slid his thumb into his mouth. "You can go with her to the dining domit, but then you need to come back and remain here with her. Is that understood?"

Ben's thumb popped when he tugged it from his mouth. "Where goin', Mommy?" He leaned against Fluffy who watched the guys with tail-wagging glee.

A few caught the flash of her fangs and backed toward the door.

"I need to show the berry big guys how to build something special," I said.

"Come wit you?" he said, his lower lip trembling.

His expression pretty much ripped my heart out. He'd been sick. He could get sick again.

I should stay with him.

The second I thought the last, I put on the brakes.

Here I went again, clinging. Narcial would take very good care of my boys. I needed to start trusting others.

"You have to stay with Will and Narcial but I won't be gone long," I said firmly—the firmness for me more than my children.

"Have you younglings heard about the time Bruge stole a narlesk and rode it to the top of Escarp Peak?" Narcial asked, luring them away from me.

I wanted to hear this tale.

Her grin my way told me she'd share later.

"Tell us," Will said, bouncing around in front of her.

"Tell," Ben said, distracted.

I stooped down and kissed their cheeks, urging him to join Narcial. "I'll be back before you miss me."

Ben watched me over his shoulder before scooting forward to stand beside Will and gaze raptly at Narcial.

Fluffy followed, perhaps to hear the story herself.

Narcial's grin took over her face, reminding me of how few children there were here. The Ferlaern had lost so much, just like us.

"Let's head out." I wove through the guys to the door and went outside with them trooping behind me.

Bruge waited outside.

"Are you ready?" He lifted my plans. They weren't much, just drawings I made back on Earth of very simple mills. I wasn't sure I'd ever have the chance to use them, and I knew the Ferlaern didn't have factories or smithies to make needed parts, but a tiny part of me hoped there would be a chance to bring some of Earth's favorite bakery treats to Ferlaern, even if only on a small scale.

First, bread. Next week? Well, I didn't want to get ahead of myself.

"I am," I said with a grin.

"Where were you last night?" he asked quietly while the guys watched.

One chuckled, though I had no idea why. It seemed whenever Bruge and I were together, someone was snickering.

"Last night?" I asked.

"Zetar…" He huffed and cut a gaze to the guys who struggled to contain their humor. "It would appear my warriors are trying to be helpful with a task I wish to do myself."

"What do you mean?"

"It has to do with…" He scowled at them again. "I will handle this alone, do you understand?"

Zetar nodded but elbowed Frelz. The two males grinned at each other.

"Alone," Bruge repeated until their grins fled.

Such an odd conversation. "As for last night, Ben was sick. He spent the evening vomiting."

"Poor youngling," he said. "There is an herb we use when someone's belly churns. I will show it to you in case you ever need it."

"That would be great."

"Wait here?" he asked. He ducked through our door flap at my nod, returning a few minutes later.

"Everything okay in there?"

"I…" Bruge grinned. "Last night, I carved a small droog for Ben."

"You did that for him? That's sweet of you."

"I am not the best at carving, but I hope it cheers him. I will craft something different for Will."

I spontaneously hugged him, and the guys chuckled

some more. One of these days, I was going to pin Zetar down and find out what was so funny.

When we pulled apart, we started toward the plain above the village with the guys following. Their footsteps thumped on the beaten path, and they chatted about this and that. Thankfully, the chuckles had faded.

"Tonight is the auction," Bruge said. His spine tightened as if he girded himself for battle. "I am prepared. Are you?"

He sounded so...resolved. Did he worry about his offer? "My basket is ready, if that's what you mean."

"I mean are you prepared to make your selection?"

"You mean which offering I'll pick?" I needed to ask Josie about the rules about that again as I'd forgotten.

"You will be amazed by what I will offer," he said.

"What could it be?" I teased, walking close enough to him, I could lean against his arm.

"You shall see. It will astonish you. Please you. You will not be able to resist."

This, I had to see. "I've never been good with waiting, so tell me."

"I am not allowed, but it will be worth the wait."

Why did my mind take this in a sexual direction? It wasn't like he would pull out his cock and offer me that, right?

Oh, shit. What if he did? It could be an ancient Ferlaern tradition.

My gaze went to his pants, and I swore something stirred. Well, I was stirring, too, but I would restrain my urge to kiss him until we were alone.

If we were ever alone.

There would be no making out with ten warriors watching.

We reached the plain, and I stopped and held out my

hand for the oven plans while the males crowded around me.

"We're going to build four ovens with the rocks you collected." I gestured the ginormous piles, marveling that they'd collected this many in such a short period of time. "I think we should clear an area outside the narlesk path, however. We don't want them potentially damaging the structures."

Zetar nodded. "This is wise." He waved to our left. "Over there?"

I surveyed the flat area. "Perfect. We might need a fence around them, too, to keep other creatures from wandering close."

"We will do this," he said with a fist to his chest.

"We'll mortar the stones together with mud from the bank of the river," I said.

We discussed how best to construct the ovens and where to place them. The guys began clearing the ground, and I helped for a while before Bruge and I left them to finish.

We walked to my domit.

"I'm worried," I said along the way.

"Why?"

"What if I can't bring this together? You're relying on me." The Clans could starve if I failed.

"We have many sources of food," he said, his arm dropping onto my shoulders. "Whatever contribution you make will be welcome but know right now, we will take care of each other no matter what."

"You mean we're in this together, and it's not just me trying to carry the burden?"

Stopping on Main Street, he cupped my face and stroked my cheeks with his thumbs. "I understand feeling responsible."

"You're a warlord," I said. "Responsibility is in your bones. How long have you worn the powldron?"

"For eight cycles," he said, his fingers tracing the wood and steel armor fused to his shoulder.

"Does it hurt?" I'd heard very little about this other than a powldron was passed down from one warlord to his son or daughter. If the powldron accepted this person, it would meld to their skin. They could take it off at night but wore it most of the time. It became a part of them, and rumor had it the powldron could lend them strength during a time of need.

"Not at all," he said in such a light tone, I couldn't help but believe him.

Would I want to fuse with something like this? I wasn't sure. I hadn't decided if I wanted to bond with a trundier, either.

Voices rang out and we passed my domit, continuing to the other end of town where we stopped at the fence separating the trundier area from our homes. I gripped the rail and watched Missy, Rayne's six-year-old daughter, run across the open area with a small hatchling trundier following.

"Yes, like that," Durran said, standing not far from Missy.

I was going to miss Rayne when we parted at the end of this season, her going with Durran to join the Willen Clan while I returned to the Suthen Clan. Maybe we could arrange some gatherings.

I peeked at Bruge standing beside me, cheering on Missy as she stopped and raced toward the trundier. My gulp slipped out as the creature came to an abrupt stop and dropped down onto its front knees in front of her.

Missy leaped up and grabbed the hatchling's spine

spike and used it as leverage to scramble up onto the trundier's back. Once seated, she lifted her arms in the air.

"I did it," she squealed as Durran strolled over to her. He patted her back and gave the trundier effusive praise.

"We have located a cluster of slidarns living in a cavern not far from here," Bruge said. "My warriors are setting traps that will capture but not harm them. We will take three from each ten and release the rest. We must preserve the flock in their natural environment in case we need to gather more." He nudged his head back toward the village. "I have allocated three domits for the creatures, but plan to build a fenced area behind where they can roam and lay eggs. If they reproduce as well while fenced as they do in the wild, we will soon be overrun with eggs."

"Can we eat slidarns?"

"Their flesh?" His frown cleared, and he grinned. "Yes. Another source of food for our people."

"We're changing," I said. The Ferlaern were migratory, and they'd continue to move each season, but it was good that they could adapt. "I hope that's okay."

"It is amazing." His hand slid along my lower back, and heat flamed through me. "One of the Earthling females brought seeds. She's working with warriors to construct a large garden. Our ways may be different, but this is for the better. If we only do things one way, we risk our future."

"Adaptation helps ensure survival."

He nodded.

"I should go back," I said, watching as Missy slid off the trundier. She gave the creature a treat, then waved for the beast to rise. Under Durran's direction, she inspected the trundier's wings and feet.

We turned and strolled to my domit.

Grunts and what sounded like a struggle echoed from inside. I paused on the path, frowning.

When the sounds grew in volume, and I swore I heard a yelp from Ben, I leaped forward, shoving the flap to step inside.

Bruge's mother sat on the floor with Will and Ben lying on either side of her.

She leaned forward, pressing a hand over each of my son's mouths.

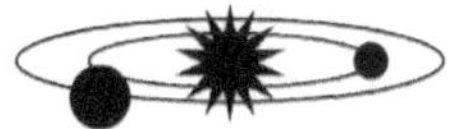

Bruge

"What the hell are you doing?" Alexa cried, stomping forward. She wrenched my mother's hands away from the younglings and tugged them up off the floor to gather them close.

Ben giggled. "Mommy, no. Play wit Irella."

Fluffy stood beside the sofa, her tail sweeping back and forth hard enough it made a table shift when it hit.

"How can anyone call smothering children playing?" Alexa half-sobbed. She slumped to the floor and rocked her sons, tears streaking down her face.

"I was teaching them our ways," Mother said stiffly. She rose, towering over Alexa and the younglings. "But if you do not wish this, I will leave." She turned to me. "I have tried but…" Her thick brow wedges lifted. "This is why I oppose mating with Earthlings. They do not understand our ways and they are not willing to learn."

"Give Alexa a chance," I said softly.

"Did I not just do so? I came here when Narcial had to rush to help a warrior wounded by a narlesk." Her arms flipped up. "Did I have to do this? No. Yet, I did, in an effort to understand the younglings my son indicated he may wish to call his own."

Alexa's head lifted. "You said that?" she cried.

I nodded, expecting—no, hoping—she'd be happy to hear this, but her tears only fell faster.

"Bruge…"

My mother's brows lifted higher. "See?" She stomped around me and shoved the door flap to the side. "I know when I'm not wanted."

"No," Alexa said, and my mother paused partway out the door. "I'm sorry if I've overreacted. I tend to do that with my boys. You see…" Shifting Ben and Will to the side, she stood. "My husband died of the disease, and since then, I've been afraid something horrible would happen to my sons, that they'd die, too. So I hover. I freely admit I sometimes hover too much."

My mother sniffed but didn't leave. I kept my mouth closed, waiting to see what would happen.

"I'm sorry I jumped all over you without looking closely at the situation first," Alexa said. "Could you explain? You must understand how this appeared."

"It is common to teach younglings how to be silent when a predator is near," I offered. "We cause no harm, but if a child cries out, everyone is in danger."

"That makes sense, but…" Alexa shook her head, and tears shimmered in her eyes again. "I thought she was hurting them."

"I would never hurt a youngling, not even an Earthling child," my mother said stiffly. "Why would you think this of me?"

"Maybe because you already hurt me," Alexa said.

Mother growled. "You know why I behave in this way."

Alexa snorted. "Not really. Would you care to explain?"

My mother stomped closer to Alexa. "It is common to teach younglings in this manner. We do so as a game because we have found the lesson is more easily retained. I cannot believe you, who claims you are overprotective of your sons, have not instilled this basic lesson in your boys. It is a disgrace."

"We don't have predators on Earth like on Ferlaern," Alexa said, her hands spreading out at her sides. She shook her head. "I guess that doesn't really matter. I apologize for overreacting, for not waiting to see what you were doing before I jumped in and snatched my boys away."

"I see," my mother said. When I caught her eye and lifted my brows, her growl slipped out. Her shoulders loosened. "And I..." Her eyes pinched shut before opening again. "I apologize for not explaining what I was doing the munette you arrived." She pivoted sharply. "I must go. You are here now and can care for your younglings yourself." She flicked the door flap aside and left, the flap smacking closed behind her.

"I'm sorry," Alexa said, sitting on the floor and wrapping her arms around Ben and Will who'd watched the entire exchange with big eyes. "I thought we might be forming some sort of truce, but it seems we're not."

"I understand." I dropped to the floor beside her and tugged all three of them onto my lap.

Will giggled and stared up at me. "Big Bruge."

"Big," Ben said solemnly. He held up a carved droog the size of his fist. "Love Fluffy."

It looked exactly like Fluffy, and my heart stung because he'd taken time to do this for Ben.

"I cannot imagine what you thought when you saw her with her hand over Will and Ben's mouths," I said, tempted to suggest my mother only had good intentions, but did she?

I would ask her why she chose *this* trick to teach the younglings when she must have heard us arriving outside. If she did this to bring trouble, I would speak with her. Again.

She and Alexa needed to settle this between themselves, but I would not allow my mother to cause Alexa pain.

"I'll find her and apologize again," Alexa said.

The younglings struggled and I released them. They leaped up and skipped across the room, Ben chasing Will into their room. Wrestling and laughter rang out.

Alexa turned to face me and twisted her legs around my waist. I liked her here, where she belonged.

"I want to get along with everyone in the village, but especially with her," Alexa said.

"My mother can be a challenge."

Leaning back, she smirked. "So can my boys. I've learned a trick or two with them that might work with her."

"I will help in any way I can."

"Perhaps I should do this alone. She and I haven't exchanged more than a few words, and each has been fueled by anger. I imagine if we talk, we'll find a way toward respect if not friendship." She tipped her head back to look up at me. "She's your mother. If…" She sighed. "I don't really know where this is going, but she's your mother, and I want to get along with her. I'll leave it at that."

I wrapped my arms around her and held her.

"What will you place in your basket?" I asked.

She smiled and shook a finger in my face. "You know we're not supposed to tell."

I growled. "I wish to spend this time with you. Whenever we try to be alone, something happens." Even Zetar and my warrior's attempts to push us together were not working out as they should.

Her laughter rose between us. "It does seem that way, doesn't it?" She wiggled in my lap, and my cock responded, like always. "Maybe you should tell me what you plan to offer tonight."

I mimicked her tone and even shook my finger in her face. "You know we are not supposed to tell."

"Then it looks like we're at a stalemate, Bruge," she said. Leaning forward, she sucked my finger into her mouth and swirled her tongue across the tip.

Just like that, flames erupted inside me. The culier threads on my cock stiffened. My fuckin' cock stiffened. I ached to bury it inside her.

As if the fates heard my thoughts, Ben and Will raced from their room and over to us.

"We wanna play," Will said.

"Play," Ben echoed.

"Sitting is boring," Will added.

It wasn't boring a munette ago. It was… I sighed.

Thwarted again.

"The phrase you're seeking is cock blocked," Alexa said with a snicker.

"That is me, completely blocked."

"Maybe not forever?" she said with a wink. "Win my basket tonight, and we'll see what happens."

The sun set, and we gathered in the community domit.

"Welcome," Piper called out. She started to climb onto a chair to see all the tall males crowding close, but Garek lifted her onto his shoulders. She clung to his horns and grinned. "Well. This is fun." Her smile swept across the room and the numerous available males waiting eagerly to see if their bids were chosen. "As you know, to enter the auction, you were first allowed to examine the contents of each basket."

I had, and I believed I knew which was Alexa's. What if I was wrong?

She stood with the other available females, lined up behind the baskets. Her gaze met mine, and I read a hint of worry there. Was she concerned she'd choose someone else's offer or that I'd bid on the wrong one? I'd spent sunslices dreaming up the task I'd bid, one she'd know was mine. Only now did I worry she wouldn't understand my clue.

"After you inspected the baskets, you were asked to select one and place your bid with Narcial," Piper continued. "All of you will not win. There are many available Ferlaern and only a few handfuls of unmatched Earthling women."

"Pick," someone shouted, though I wasn't sure who.

Saldarn laughed loudly, and I wondered why. While this was a game for entertainment, Piper's words weren't funny.

"As you know, the baskets are on display over there." Piper pointed to the cloth-draped baskets sitting on a table along one wall. "When the basket is named, the offering bids will be announced."

"Me," Narcial said with a flash of her fangs. She poked her chest. "I will be announcing the bids."

"At that time," Piper said. "Whoever crafted the basket will step forward. She will enjoy the contents with you tonight." A frown stole her lingering humor. "I want to remind you that this is a game. It's supposed to be fun. We ask each of you to keep the spirit of the event in mind. You offered a service, and we'll call it due soon, letting you know who will receive it and how you can deliver."

Anticipation burrowed deeply inside me, making me twitchy, but I held myself still. This was one evening. If I did not win Alexa's basket, there would be other opportunities for us to be alone.

"Without further ado," Piper said. "Let's start calling the numbers."

"Numbers?" Saldarn asked. He staggered toward Piper, but his friend, Trudar, latched onto his arm, holding him back. "What numbers do you speak of?"

"I mean the number on the tag pinned to the basket," Piper said.

We universally turned and stared in that direction. There was a tag on the baskets, each with a different symbol, but I did not know what the mark meant.

"Okay, so I guess I should've thought of that earlier," Piper said. "The basket closest to me has a number one on the tag. Then, for the subsequent tags, two, three, four, etcetera, all the way to ten, as there are still ten single Earthling females seeking mates from among you."

Garek huffed. "Winning the basket does not mean you win the female for mating." His voice lifted. "If your offer is chosen, you are granted one evening to share the basket's contents with this female, and that is all. Nothing else. I ask you to respect this."

I wanted to push forward to the front, but location would not make a difference.

"As I was saying, let's get started, shall we?" Piper said. "For basket number one, would the lady who crafted the awesome contents step forward."

Josie left Alexa's side and strode over to stand behind the basket. "Just so you know," she said with a laugh. "I'm a nurse, not a cook, so you might end up gnawing on your fingers."

No one made a sound as we pondered her words.

"Talk about a tough audience. Just…" Her lips thinned as she stared into the crowd. I followed her gaze to Zetar, who scowled right back at her. So…was she the one he said he disliked but who he couldn't stop thinking about? "Anyway, would you call out the bids, Narcial?"

Narcial stepped forward, her chest puffing with pride. "We have many offers for this basket, despite its interesting contents." She smirked at Josie.

"Hey, it's not that bad!" Josie tipped the basket forward, revealing starcrest, a fruit picked from trees growing on the bank of the river, a bound package that could contain almost anything but looked as if it came from the dining domit, and a flask of liquid. "What do we have for bids, Narcial?"

"First offer?" A hush fell across the room. "An offer to build a bathing room in someone's domit!"

"Oh!" Josie cried. "If I pick that one, do I win it?"

"The service will be provided to whoever has the greatest need," Narcial said, her smirk growing. "But if you enjoy your evening with whoever bid, perhaps you can persuade him to add such an addition onto your own domit?"

"Great idea. What else?" Josie asked.

"Someone offered to plant a vegetable garden behind a domit." Narcial continued, naming the various tasks offered. "A ride over the plain on a narlesk." After fifteen offers, she bowed. "And now, Josie, you must choose. Which will be selected and gifted to our community? Who will share your basket this evening?"

"Hmm." Josie frowned, tapping her chin with her finger. "I pick… The ride on a narlesk!"

Zetar stepped forward and even I could read the uncertainty in his hitched stride.

"Fuck, no," Josie cried, color filling her brown cheeks. She spun and raced across the room and out the front door of the community domit.

Zetar growled, watching as she fled.

"Go after her," Narcial said, snatching up the basket and handing it to Zetar. "Go!"

Zetar dropped the basket on the floor and stormed to the back door of the domit. He shifted the flap aside and the thud of his retreating footsteps followed.

"Well, that went over well," Piper said. She slid off Garek and stood with her back pressed against him. A fake smile rose on her face. "Shall we move on to basket number two, Narcial?"

Each basket was distributed, and each couple left the domit with eager strides. Soon, only one basket remained.

Alexa's.

I'd chosen the one I knew had to be hers. Would she do the same with my offer?

Narcial announced the other offers while a smaller group of males waited, their feet shifting with unease. There was still a sizeable crowd hoping to spend the evening with Alexa.

My guts burned, but I kept my lips pressed tightly together. I would stand by the final decision even if it meant watching as she left with someone else.

"And the final offer is a complete sunslice of youngling care so the female can do whatever she pleases."

"Who would want that?" Saldarn snarled. "That is not a service anyone would choose."

Narcial scowled. "This shows how little you know

females, Saldarn. But enough. It is time for Alexa to choose who she will do hanging with for the evening."

Alexa stepped forward, her steps slow as if she were taking time to think.

"I choose…" Her sorrow-filled gaze met mine. "I choose…"

Alexa

"A sunslice of youngling care," I announced.

I was taking a chance as the offers were all excellent, but I remembered my conversation with Bruge when I first found Fluffy, how I said it would be wonderful to have even one free hour for myself to lounge in a tub and wash my hair.

He was the kind of guy who'd remember something like that.

This had to be his offer.

Bruge grinned, confirming my suspicion.

Warmth filled me, swirling from my breasts to my belly, diving deeply.

"I'll take the boys for the evening," Piper said with a smile. She strode over to me and held out her hands. "Will? Ben? How would you like to have a slumber party with Noah tonight?"

"Yeah!" Will cried with joy.

Ben hopped in place; his face wreathed with happiness.

Bruge scooped up my basket—with my solitary offering inside—and dropped the handle over his arm.

Piper—acting as the Pied Piper—led my boys away with a wink and a cheerful promise to deliver my sons back to me by late tomorrow morning.

Bruge held his hand out to me. "I believe we are finally being granted a few munettes alone and it is not facilitated by my warriors."

"What does that mean?"

"They have been trying to… I'm not sure of the term."

Oh. "Fix us up?"

He frowned.

"Get us together," I said.

His face smoothed. "Yes, that is it. I spoke with them, and they will stop."

"It's kind of cute." Imagine, his warriors playing matchmaker. I chuckled.

"Forget my warriors," he grumbled.

I saluted him. "Yes, Sir!"

He rolled his eyes, and I bet he learned that move from Savvy.

"Are you willing to take whatever might arise from the evening, Alexa?" he asked, and I swore I heard his heart in his voice.

When had I fallen for this guy? Maybe when he coaxed Ben into doing something first, rather than following his brother. Or when he sang the goodnight song for my boys. Or when he knew that the solitary piece of flatbread in my basket had been made by me.

All of them combined, actually. They wrapped around him like a big red bow.

It was time to tug the knot free and release him.

"Let's get out of here, Bruge," I said with a grin. "Before some new disaster happens to keep us apart."

Holding hands, we rushed from the community domit

with Narcial's cackle ringing out behind us. Outside the building, Bruge scooped me up and with the basket dangling from his other arm, he raced across the village.

"If this is your abduction, don't stop for anything," I yelled as I clung to him, my arms around his neck, my heart racing double time.

"You will well and truly be abducted, Alexa," he called out.

When we reached the trundier pen, he didn't stop. He leaped over it, his laughter trailing behind him.

At Bruge's call, Nykas sank down to the ground. Bruge jumped onto the creature's back and lowered me to the beast in front of him. His arm looped around my waist.

"Should I be protesting this?" I asked with a laugh.

"Why would you?"

"You're abducting me."

He leaned forward and kissed my cheek. "You want me to abduct you."

I fell back into his embrace. "I do."

Nykas jumped up at Bruge's signal, wings extending. He flapped hard, taking us into the night sky.

"Can you see?" I called as the huge trundier soared away from the village. The wind stung my eyes and whipped my hair around me. I tipped my head back and bellowed out my joy.

"Can you not see?" he said.

I giggled, a silly sound for a mom of two boys, but damn, I felt free for the first time in… Well, in a long time.

My body thrilled at the thought of what would come next.

Come…

I snickered and savored the feel of Bruge's arms around me. My shoulder pinched for a second, but I brushed off the feeling. Must be a twinge from smacking it against something earlier.

We flew for what felt like an hour, but who needed to pay attention to time when you spent it with someone you…loved. Yes, I loved Bruge. I couldn't wait to tell him.

Nykas dove downward, and my heart raced in my throat. The great beast landed on soft soil and dropped down so we could dismount.

"Where are we?" I asked, peering around. Clouds covered the moons tonight, and I couldn't see more than a few feet in front of my face.

"Let me show you." Bruge slid off Nykas and held his hand out to me.

Somehow, he still held the basket which was a bit ridiculous as it contained almost nothing. It was a wonder anyone but him bid on it.

"You knew the basket was mine," I said as I dropped off Nykas and into Bruge's arms.

"Just as you knew the offered service was mine."

"You remembered," I said, wrapping my arms around him.

"How could I forget? For tonight, you will not be alone, however. You will not have time to poo your hair or apply a gloss to your nails as I've heard Earthlings enjoy. That is for another day."

"The services will be offered to the community."

"Do you not know?" he said with a flash of his tusks. "This offer is open for you whenever you wish for it. I will stay with the younglings, and you will do the poo with your hair. You will lounge in a warm bath, and you will gloss whatever part of your body you wish."

"Bruge," I said, trying not to laugh about putting poo in my hair. "That's the most romantic thing anyone has ever said to me."

"Is it?" He took my hand and tugged me away from Nykas. "Then let me see if I can offer you something even better."

27

Bruge

I wanted Alexa. Desperately. But even more than my own satisfaction, I wanted to give her pleasure.

As I led her down the narrow trail weaving through the thick grass, I told my body to be patient. Tonight was for her. Tomorrow? We would see at the next sunslice.

"Where are we going?" she whispered, scooting up close to me.

"Why speak so quietly?" I asked in a normal tone.

"Predators, remember? Your mother implied they were everywhere."

"There are none here. If there were, they would've fled when Nykas arrived."

"Will your trundier stay around?" she asked, the tension leaving her voice.

"He will." He might leave to hunt, but he would return.

We reached our destination and I stopped, tugging my mate close. I wrapped my arms around her and held her close while she gazed around.

The clouds cooperated and revealed our moons, which shone light down on our destination.

Alexa gasped. "It's so pretty here." She left my embrace and walked forward, toward the gleaming pool in the center of the oasis.

Trees grew along the banks of the pool except for one side where a small, gleaming golden beach waited.

"Are we swimming?" she asked in awe.

"We can." I followed her, remaining close, though as I said, nothing would come near with Nykas around. Or me for that matter.

"I'd love to swim. It was hot today, and I feel sticky."

"Take your clothing off, then," I said eagerly.

She whirled around and grinned while tugging her shirt over her head. She tossed it aside as well as the garment she wore beneath.

I heard about breasts, and I had to admit, when I first watched them bounce on the Earthling females' chests, I was repulsed.

Then, I felt reluctant fascination.

Now, I ached to touch Alexa's. Suck on the rosy buds in the center of each.

My weapons straps dropped to the ground with a clatter.

"You have…" Frowning, Alexa came closer. She stopped in front of me and traced the symbol on my shoulder. "This means…"

"You're my maelstrom mate. My second heart beats only for you, love."

"Love…" she sighed. "I feel the same."

I kissed her quickly. "Mate."

"Bruge." Tears glistened in her eyes, and she rubbed her arms, her fingers gliding up to cup her shoulders. "I don't have a matching symbol. Your second heart could be beating for someone else."

"Then what is this, mate?" I asked, leaning forward to kiss the mark on her shoulder. My heart had filled to overflowing when I saw it in the moonlight.

"Wait, what?" Twisting, she peered down at her shoulder before she grinned at me. "Where did that come from?"

"From us." Taking her hands, I pulled her close. Her bare flesh against mine made my hearts race faster than a herd of narlesks on a rampage.

"Show me how it can be, Bruge. Please?"

I lifted my powldron, something I rarely did even to sleep. It made a subtle sucking sound as it released. After carefully lowering it beside my weapons' straps, I straightened.

I reached for the fastener at the top of her pants and pressed, pulled, and tried to pry the damn device apart.

A soft laugh shot out of her. "Let me?" With a twist of her wrist, she undid the fastening. She shimmied the pants down over her generous hips and then slipped out of the silky garment beneath.

"Here I am," she said, her spine tight. "Do whatever you want with me."

"Who can resist an offer like that?" I shucked my pants and stood before her, feeling oddly vulnerable.

"You're amazing," she said, her gaze gliding from my chest to my abs then on to my cock. It twitched upward, the culier strand coiling and weaving around the tip coated with precum. She frowned. "What…?"

My breath jarred in my lungs. "Is something wrong?" Did she find me lacking?

"Not at all. It's just…" Her hand reached out but

stopped before touching. "I've never seen anything like this before."

"A cock?"

"No, these." Her fingertip glided along a culier strand, and it coiled around her finger. "Whoa. This is amazing." She looked up at me with joy and excitement shining in her eyes. "What do they do?"

"Stroke your inner walls."

"And this?" Her finger dipped close to the base of my cock.

"You have found the culier strand made especially for you."

She grinned slyly. "Aren't they all made for me?"

"This one will suck on your clit."

Her jaw dropped. "Fuck."

"It could fuck you as well, but I think this," I fisted my shaft, "will bring you greater pleasure."

"I want to feel it all, Bruge." She backed toward the water but extended her hand. "Come with me. We have tonight, correct?"

I nodded and paced after her, unable to resist her lure. I'd abducted her. Now it was time to seduce her.

"Let's not waste a bit of tonight," she said, stepping into the pool. Water lapped over her legs, her thighs, and her belly. She dove forward, submerging, and when she popped up above the water, she slicked back her hair.

I plunged in after her, swimming beneath the water until I reached her. My fingers glided up her body as I rose to the surface.

My breathing raged from my lungs and my fever had nothing to do with holding my breath a few munettes. I wanted her. More than anything.

She wrapped her legs around my waist and ground herself against my cock.

"I'm tempted to take you hard and fast, mate, because I fear someone, or something, will interrupt us."

"Do it," she said, her eyes hooded, and her head tilted back.

"Absolutely not."

She pouted and pushed harder against me, trying to place the tip of my cock at her opening. "Why not?"

"We have tonight, and I am going to savor it as if it were my last." Holding her still against my chest, I carried her to a boulder partly submerged in the water. Mossy liketern grew across the top and I knew from standing on it to jump into the water as a youngling that liketern was soft.

Laying her down on her back, I tugged her hips close to the edge and spread her legs, placing one on each of my shoulders.

Stooping forward, I teased her clit with the tip of my tail.

I grinned up at her. "Forget sleep, mate. I plan to fuck you all night."

28

Alexa

My blood roared through me. I wanted Bruge and I wanted him now.

While his tail stroked my clit, his hot, scratchy tongue teased inside my folds.

I keened, not embarrassed at all when my voice echoed in the oasis.

"Bruge," I cried, latching onto his horns.

He grunted and lifted his head. "Keep doing that, mate, and you will drive me out of my mind."

"Maybe I want you acting feral."

"Not yet." His head lowered, and he slid his tongue inside me. It was longer than it looked. The tip glided across my G-spot, and I couldn't help it. I jerked my hips upward, seeking more.

I held onto his horns, my body overcome, as he licked my inside walls. The end of his tail tightened around my clit, and I swore, it vibrated.

I was soon a writhing mess, splayed out for him to feast on.

He licked and sucked and pumped his tail inside me, stroking my inner walls while my brain turned to mush.

My body tightened. I was going to come apart and only Bruge would ever be able to put me back together. As everything inside me coiled tight, I gripped his horns and yanked on them. I'd do this when I rode his huge cock.

"Alexa," he hissed, lifting his head. His dark eyes were hooded, gleaming with pleasure. "I…"

"Fuck me, Bruge," I half-bellowed. Languid heat flooded me, threatening to sweep me away. I wanted him with me when it happened.

"Yes."

He rose over me, staring down at my wide-spread legs. I must gape open, showing my pussy swollen with need. Placing the head of his cock at my opening, he propped himself over me. He dwarfed me, making me feel too tiny to take such a huge male inside.

I gripped his arms and tugged, urging him on. When he pushed forward slightly, I lifted my hips.

"I need this," I ground out. "Now."

"It will not fit," he hissed. "I saw. Even two of my fingers was almost too much. I do not want to hurt you."

"You bring this up now?" I pumped my hips up, seeking… "You're going to hurt me if you don't give me what I need."

His face loosened, and he chuckled. "Now is the time for someone to appear and ask me to help them with a task."

"Bruge." My fingers tightened on his arms. "*I* am asking you to help me with this task."

"Mate," he huffed out.

"It'll fit," I insisted. "Push hard and you'll find yourself inside."

He jerked his hips back and started to drop down, but I held him close with a tight grip on his arms.

"No way," I said. "We can do whatever we want with each other, and I want you. *All* of you."

"You must tell me if it hurts," he said solemnly.

"Take me," I said. "Everything I have."

He growled and leaning forward, nipped at my neck with his tusks. The subtle pinch seared through me.

The head of his cock slipped inside my folds and stopped.

Bruge braced himself over me, watching me as he slowly inched forward. Exquisite torture, I wasn't sure I could take much more before I exploded. Each bit of him felt better than the last.

Something stroked my inner walls and another culier strand glided over my G-spot.

He pulled back and pushed forward again, the thick bulb stretching me further. It bordered on pain, but it felt so damn good.

I spread myself wider as heat came to a boil inside me.

When he cautiously inched forward—again—I lowered my hips. He moved toward me, and I jerked up, taking all of him inside.

His groan echoed around us, and I swore his eyes rolled back in his head.

"Alexa," he growled. Pulling out, he pushed back hard.

"Yes," I cried, clinging to him, tightening my inner walls around him.

Muscles straining and cords standing out sharply on his neck, he rocked against me, giving me everything he had. He leaned over and bit down on my shoulder. I shrieked at the amazing sensation.

His hips pumped, and the culier strand at the base of

his cock latched onto my clit. When it made a sucking motion, I cried out.

My body tightened and I shuddered as I succumbed to the best orgasm of my life.

We slid into the water some time later. The moons continued to rise overhead as Bruge gently washed me. He cradled me and lay back, floating with me resting across his chest.

Peace settled within me, plus a burning need to claim this male for all time.

"I'm going to take you up on your offer," I said softly. "If it's still open."

My fingers walked down his abs to his cock. It lay rigid against him, and a culier thread coiled around my finger, tugging gently.

"You may have my body whenever you please." His chest shook with his laugh.

I tightened my fingers around his cock, stroking him. "That wasn't what I meant about an offer." What if he'd changed his mind? "I want to move into your domit. Me and the boys, that is. If you still want me. Us."

"Alexa." His legs dropped down, and he lifted me up for a long, lingering kiss that turned my blood to liquid fire. "I will want you forever. Nothing would honor me more than claiming you to the world as my maelstrom mate. As for Will and Ben, I would be equally honored to name them as my younglings."

Tears made my eyes sting. "Bruge." I cupped his shoulders and kissed him, sinking into him and the joy he made me feel.

He carried me to the shore and lowered me to the

ground, his mouth remaining locked to mine. His tongue stroked mine, entwining.

Kissing down my neck, he reached my breasts. He sucked one nipple into his mouth while his amazing tail parted my thighs. Fuck. We'd barely finished, and I wanted him again already.

My nipples hardened, and my clit ached. His tail stroked me, and I gushed with warmth. But when I thought his tail would glide inside me, he lifted his head.

"Roll over, love," he said hoarsely. "Show me your glorious ass."

"What are you going to do to my glorious ass?" I asked, feeling impish.

"Admire it. Kiss it. And then make you cry out my name."

"I'm on board with that," I said, flipping over faster than I ever had before.

He lifted my hips and spread my body wide. Then his tongue stroked my wet folds. I could tell I dripped for him, and he seemed eager to lick up each and every drop.

His tail stroked my breasts while his tongue worked wonders between my legs. I was soon a writhing mess, begging him for whatever he wanted to give. He rose over me and placed his cock at my entrance. A shove, and he was seated inside. No more pussy footing around, saying he wouldn't fit. We'd proven we were a perfect match in more ways than one.

While his tail rubbed my clit, his cock plundered inside me. He rode me, hard and fast as I begged, until we tumbled into ecstasy together.

Sadly, when morning came, we had to return to the village. We mounted Nykas and flew home.

Bruge walked with me to Piper's domit to collect Ben and Will.

"Mommy," Will cried, rushing over to greet me.

Ben hopped up from where he was playing with Noah on the floor by the sofa and barreled around the couch, his little legs churning. When I stooped down, he leaped into my arms.

"Missed you, Mommy," he said by my ear. His arms splayed wide, one almost hitting me in the boobs. "This much."

I hugged him again, giving Will an equal number of kisses, passing them back and forth until my boys were squirming and squealing with laughter.

When I released them, they remained near, each leaning against one of my legs.

"They had a fantastic time," Piper said. "How about you?" Her grin told me she knew very well what we did while we were gone, and the gleam in her eyes told me she approved.

"Wonderful." I straightened and leaned back against Bruge. His arms went around me to stroke Ben and Will's heads. "I'm moving."

"Ah, so it's like that, is it?" she said with glee. She hopped back and forth, her hands clasped to her chest. "I hoped this would happen! We all…"

"You all tried to get us together, didn't you? Bruge mentioned his warriors, but you were in on it, too?" I aked with a laugh. "Life just kept getting in the way."

"Fate is a mysterious wench, and she loves to twist us into knots, amiright?" Piper asked.

"For sure."

"Where moving, Mommy?" Ben asked, tipping his head back to look up at me.

"We're going to live with Bruge," I said. "What do you think of that, boys?"

Ben bounced, giving me a huge smile, while Will raced around to Bruge and hugged his knee.

"I gotta pack," Will said in complete seriousness. "Want my toys."

"Fluffy, too," Ben said. "Right?"

"Yes," I said. "Fluffy, too." I peeked up at Bruge. "You didn't know what you were in for when you picked me, now did you?"

His arms tightened around me. "I could not ask for anything more."

29

Alexa

I t didn't take long to move our things, and we were soon settled in Bruge's big domit. The boys had their own room. Fluffy had a blanket in a corner of the main living area. And Bruge's bed was covered in furs and large enough for two.

Of course, we could've gotten by with a twin bed as I spent most of the time lying on top of him. Well, when I wasn't riding him, that is.

I loved my new life with my mate, and I couldn't imagine it getting any better.

So, when Bruge's mother came scratching on my door, I was more than willing to meet her halfway.

"Come in," I said cheerfully as I encouraged her to step inside.

Fluffy raised her head and stared at Irella before dropping her head back onto her paws.

"I just put the boys down for a nap," I said. "We can kick back, put our feet up, and have…" Well, there was no alcohol in Ferlaern. Piper would call it a dry town. "We can have a cup of tea." I think. A device similar to a tea kettle sat on the counter. It was a plant, naturally, as there was no electricity here. But when I put water from a jug into the plant's center and rubbed the outer layer, the water heated.

If only we had something similar to coffee beans…

"I do not wish to have tea. I do not want to kick anything." Irella smirked, telling me she might be okay with kicking me, however.

This time, she might find me returning the gesture should she choose to deliver it. To play it safe, I rounded the sofa and sat in a squishy chair. I wasn't sure what plant the furniture was made from, but it was soft like the memory foam leaves the Ferlaern slept on when they traveled. A few Ferlaern crafted the furniture, gifting it to whoever had need.

Fluffy rose and came over to sit beside me for pats.

"Why are you here, then?" I asked Irella as I stroked Fluffy's silky ears. "As you said, you don't want to have tea or kick anything." I smirked, enjoying the conversation, if nothing else.

She heaved a sigh, and her lips compressed together before she spoke. "You live with my son."

"Yes. We're maelstrom mates." I nudged my shirt to the side and proudly showed her my symbol. I could tell her we loved each other, but would she understand? While I assumed she cared for Bruge in some way, she obviously didn't love him enough if she wasn't willing to step back and let him be with the person he loved.

"When did this come about?" she asked, inching forward.

I leaned back in the chair and propped my feet on the coffee table. "When he abducted me after the silent basket auction."

Her lips thinned. "I see."

"You still haven't told me why you're here."

Another heavy sigh slipped from her lungs. "If you are his mate, I will need to…" She winced, telling me this wasn't easy for her.

"You seem like a controlling person," I offered. "I don't imagine you like seeing others, especially Bruge, run his own life."

"There are Ferlaern females he would be better matched with."

"Is it because I'm not Ferlaern?" I asked, striving to sound pleasant. Instead, I felt like I spoke through a mouth full of broken glass. "Or because I have children?"

She actually looked shocked. "Younglings are precious no matter their species."

"So why do you have a problem with Earthlings?"

"You…" She scowled.

"It's because you didn't pick me out and groom me, isn't it?"

"Of course not."

I could tell by the way her face froze; I was right. "Then why?"

"I—"

Someone scratched on the door. Frankly, I was surprised I wasn't in the middle of a heavy make out session with Bruge, since this was a timely interruption.

"Yes?" I said in a lifted voice.

Fluffy perked up from where she'd slumped on the floor beside me and padded over to the door.

"Alexa?" someone called.

I frowned, unable to place the voice. When I tucked the flap to the side, Saldarn and Trudar stood outside. "Yes?"

I had to hold Fluffy back. She wanted out, but I was hesitant to give her the freedom to roam. So far, I'd walked with her whenever she wanted to do her doggie business in the deep grass near the river. She hunted with Bruge at night.

"There is a problem with the ovens," Saldarn said. He raked his hand through his hair, infusing the faint purple strands with static electricity. They floated around him.

"What kind of problem?" I asked.

"They smoke," Trudar said.

I frowned. "Well, they're going to smoke."

Saldarn blinked slowly. "In the chamber where we will cook the bed? That would not taste good, would it?" He turned to Trudar, his fidgeting feet stirring up dust. "I do not think this bed will be satisfying. Perhaps we should tell Bruge of this problem. We'll stop construction of the ovens and find another source of food."

"No," I barked then lowered my voice. "No. I'll come look at them." I waved for them to enter, and the door flap swooshed closed behind them. "I'll need to wake my sons and bring them with us."

"I will remain here with them," Irella said firmly.

After what happened a few days ago, I told myself I wouldn't hover over my sons. Irella was Bruge's mom. He'd survived childhood and, as far as I know, she hadn't killed any children. Yet.

This was a chance to start building a better relationship with Bruge's mom. I didn't want to make him choose.

All of this ran through my mind while I nibbled on my lower lip.

"All right," I said, pressing for a smile. "Thank you. I shouldn't be long."

She rounded the sofa and sat, even propping her heels on the coffee table. "I am the kick back."

It was all I could do not to let my laughter snort out of

me. "If you'd like some tea, the plant is full." I waved to it sitting on the counter.

Irella dipped her head forward. "Thank you."

Maybe we'd find a way to get along after all.

Fluffy wanted to go with me and the guys, naturally. At the door, I stooped down and rubbed her ears.

"I'll take you out the second I get back, okay?" I said.

She groaned and sat, her tail smacking the floor.

I left, joining Saldarn and Trudar outside, and secured the flap so Fluffy couldn't follow.

"So, tell me more about this smoke problem," I said as we walked through the village and up the hill. When we crested the rise, the ovens waited on our left. No smoke, but the fire must've gone out.

"It is only one of them," Saldarn said. He took my arm and led me to the one farthest from the village. "It is inside the section where we cook the bed."

"Bread," I said distractedly. "It's called bread."

From the outside, the oven looked as it should but perhaps there was an issue on the inside. I swung the door wide and was surprised not to have heat pour out of the opening.

I tucked my head into the opening.

Someone pushed me from behind, driving me forward. My head impacted with the inside wall.

My brain spun, and a yelp burst out of me.

I was dragged out of the opening.

While Trudar tied my ankles, Saldarn stood over me, leering.

When I screamed, he slapped his big hand over my mouth.

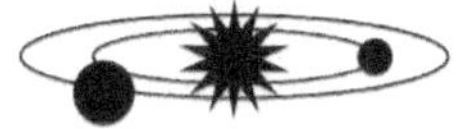

30

Bruge

My meeting with the other warlords took longer than expected, but eventually, I left the Council domit and strode back to my home. I couldn't wait to see Alexa. If the younglings still napped, I'd take her to our room and shut the door flap tight. I wanted to escape into our own world.

Instead of my loving mate, I was greeted at the door by a nearly rabid Fluffy.

I dropped to my heels and held her head still. "What is it, droog?"

"That...creature has been pacing and snarling since Alexa left," my mother said, rising from the sofa. "I am the kick back, sitting with the younglings while Alexa attends to the ovens."

"Ovens?" I asked.

"Saldarn and Trudar arrived and told her there was a problem. She went with them to investigate."

"I see." I straightened. "If you can remain here longer, I will take the droog for a walk. She is restless." Perhaps we could walk toward the ovens. I assumed I'd meet Alexa on her way back.

"I will do this. Despite what your Alexa might think, I enjoy younglings. They give an old female like me life."

"You are not old."

She came over and stroked my face. "And I am not young, but thank you." Her face creased with worry. "Are you happy, my son?"

"Very." My face stretched in a grin so big, it made my cheeks ache. "I could not be happier."

"Then I will keep trying." Her gaze traveled to the boys' room. "These younglings are…entertaining."

I chuckled. "One could say that."

"I will keep trying with them, as well." She moved quietly to their door and shifted the flap to the side to peek before returning. "They have no grandmother."

"This is true." Could she finally be softening?

"It is unfair of Alexa to bring them here, removing them from their remaining relatives on Earth."

"She did what she thought was best for her children." My mother must know I would continually defend my mate. If she tried to force me to choose, she would not like the outcome.

Mother shrugged. "I suppose." Her gaze fell on Fluffy who continued to pace in front of the door.

"The droog will bear young," Mother said.

I peered at the beast's belly, seeking bulges. "Are you sure?"

"As a mother, I know this."

"As a father, I do not." I took pride in naming Will and Ben my sons. Over the next few sunslices, I planned to teach them more about trundier care. Then when the hatchlings were born, they would be introduced and could form a bond with one. They'd be ahead of other younglings. My chest swelled with pride at the thought.

A droog bearing young, however, could be a complication. The Clans reluctantly accepted her in our midst, though if she made one threatening move, they would see her dead.

Mother huffed. "As a male you will never know this. This is the mystery locked within females. Others within our Clans may soon bear young, as well."

Alexa? We hadn't discussed children. I would be overjoyed if we had a child sharing our blood, but equally happy to raise only Will and Ben. The fates would decide, not my mother.

Fluffy whined and continued to pace.

"I should take her outside," I said. "Thank you for remaining here with the younglings."

"Perhaps I will sit with them and sing some of our traditional songs." Her head tilted. "Do you think they would like that?"

"It was something I enjoyed."

She nodded pertly. "Then I will do it. Tell Alexa I will hold off on silence games for a bit longer."

I shook my head at the humor twinkling in her eyes and stepped outside with Fluffy.

The sun hung low on the horizon, heralding night. I guided the droog toward the ovens, though she needed no encouragement. She rushed forward, and I hurried to catch up, not stopping even when a few Ferlaern called out in greeting.

We didn't meet up with Alexa on the path, but she must still be working with the ovens. They would be ready soon, as would the grain.

Would we enjoy this bread? I believed so, though many were skeptical.

I reached the top of the hill and the plain where warriors had worked on the ovens over the past sunslices to find no one there.

Fluffy ran over to an oven with an open door and poked her head inside. She backed away, reared up, and howled.

Unease raked down my spine.

"Let's go back to the village and see if Alexa went to visit a friend," I said to Fluffy.

She pivoted on her heels and bolted for the open plain. That was all I needed to know to see something was horribly wrong.

I ran after her.

31

Alexa

I woke with a pounding headache, lying on the ground with my ankles and wrists tied.

Snarls and snapping sounds behind me made my skin crawl. I carefully rolled over and stared, stunned, as Saldarn and Trudier spoke with one of the duskhorde.

I couldn't understand anything they said, but from their movements and the way the dusklen male kept leering at me with his beady red eyes, negotiations for my sale were underway.

He lifted his arms and stomped his cloven hooves, howling and clicking.

Saldarn shouted over the dusklen's voice.

His fangs gnashing, the dusklen snapped his knobby head back, his single horn spearing toward the sky. His clawed hands reached for Trudar, who backed away with horror blooming on his face. Dark fur draped down the dusklen's torso, and his sizeable cock was half-flaccid, though it twitched whenever he looked at me.

While they argued, I carefully drew up my legs and

tried to loosen the vines binding my ankles. One snapped, and I was free, but my hands were still tied.

They must've come to an agreement, because the dusklen stalked to a pile of belongings and pawed through them. He returned and handed three leather flasks to Saldarn.

Trudar chuckled and took one. He removed the cap and took a long drink from the flask. His burp rang out after.

What was he drinking?

I recalled smelling alcohol once and then Saldarn's stinky breath. When he acted belligerent, I dismissed the idea he was drunk because the Ferlaern had no liquor.

It was clear the duskhorde did. Had Saldarn and Trudar become addicted? If so, they'd do anything to get more, even trade me for three flasks of dusklen alcohol.

Trudar turned and jogged into the deep grass while Saldarn continued to speak to the dusklen. Perhaps he wasn't done negotiating after all, as there were still two flasks lying on the ground near the dusklen's things.

While they snapped and clicked at each other, I picked at the bindings at my wrists, slowly working them free. When the vine fell away, I froze, worried the dusklen or Saldarn would notice.

The dusklen stalked to the flasks and returned to Saldarn, tossing one into his arms.

Saldarn chuckled and turned to me. For one moment, what looked like regret crossed his face, but his gaze dropped to the flasks, and his spine stiffened with resolve.

The dusklen stomped toward me, grunting, his cock completely erect.

I scrambled to my feet and turned, bolting into the scruffy brush behind me.

A yelp and a bellow rang out, but I didn't stop to look. All hell broke loose behind me.

32

Bruge

As Fluffy and I drew close to where I heard voices arguing, our pace slowed. She wanted to rush forward, but I held her back with a hand in her ruff.

I pulled a weapon and crept forward through the deep grass then parted the last strands to reveal a small clearing.

Alexa lay on the ground on the opposite side while Saldarn squabbled with a dusklen. I didn't see other duskhorde around but that didn't mean a tribe of them wasn't out hunting.

Saldarn and the dusklen came to an agreement, Alexa in exchange for a few flasks of spiritte. As Saldarn tipped a flask up to drink, the dusklen chortled and strode around him, toward Alexa.

Panic widened her eyes. She sprang to her feet and ran into the dense brush with the dusklen grunting and giving chase.

Saldarn chuckled and took another drink from the flask.

A brutal concoction the duskhorde made from

fermented narlask milk, spiritte had addictive properties. Many cycles ago, we agreed as a Clan to forbid it.

It appeared Saldarn didn't agree with the Clans' decision.

I leaped from the brush and raced across the clearing.

Saldarn yelped and reeled back as I passed, but my blade skipped out, slicing across his neck. Spiritte addiction was not a death sentence, though few lived more than a cycle after tasting it. Him selling Alexa to the duskhorde was.

Deep within the brush, Alexa cried out.

My blood boiled, and I leaped into the scruff after her. Fear and rage went rabid inside me. I was desperate to reach her. Desperate to get there in time.

Beneath my powldron, my skin heated. Was this the energy I'd heard of, being fed to me by my powldron? Heat roared through me, and I went faster.

The dusklen wouldn't kill her. She was much too valuable for that. But he'd hurt her.

Thorns scratched my chest as I plunged through the thicket. I scrambled to go faster, barely avoiding tripping.

My heart was on fire. I saw red at the thought of him harming her.

When I burst from the thick brush and into another clearing, I found Alexa pressed against a tree by the dusklen. He groped her body while she whimpered and smacked his back with her hands.

I raced up to them and plunged my blade into the dusklen's spine. He twisted and my short sword snapped, breaking off at the hilt. I tossed aside the handle and yanked a knife from its sheath on my chest.

The dusklen pivoted, snarling, and I backed away, preparing to either leap on him or cut him if he rushed toward me.

Fluffy ran past me and sprang onto the dusklen, taking him down to the ground with a heavy smack. They rolled, and the dusklen scrambled to sink his claws into the droog.

Rushing to them, I slashed out with my knife, slicing deeply into the dusklen's shoulder.

Alexa left the tree and ran to the other side of the battle. She lifted a stick, bringing it down hard on the dusklen's head.

He slumped and lay unmoving while Fluffy ripped at his throat with her long teeth.

Alexa's stick dropped from her hand with a clatter, and she wavered.

I leaped over the dusklen's remains and swept Alexa up in my arms. Murmuring soothing words, I carried her some distance away from the snarling droog before dropping to the ground with her cradled on my lap.

She shuddered and lifted her face. Tears drizzled down her cheeks, and she shook her head. A sob worked its way up from deep inside her, and she burst forward, hugging me, kissing my chest.

"You came," she said. "You both did."

"Always, mate."

I rubbed her back and told her everything would be all right. That she was safe. That I loved her.

Fluffy flopped down beside us, her tail thumping steadily on the ground. When Alexa reached out to pat her, she rolled onto her back and presented her belly for rubs.

While a low purr rumbled in the droog's chest, Alexa curled up in my arms.

I explained about Sladarn and the spiritte.

"He sold me for a few flasks of alcohol." Her sigh bled out. "Trudar was in on it, too."

"I will hunt him."

"What will you do to him?"

"The same thing I did to Saldarn."

"You killed him," she said.

"I did." I would do it again this munette to protect her.

"He pretended something was wrong with the ovens, and then they grabbed and tied me."

"I am sorry."

Closing her eyes, she shook her head. "It's not your fault."

"If only I could protect you always." There were too many dangers in my world, things that could so easily harm my frail human.

Frail?

I paused. This female dealt the final blow that killed the dusklen. She was no whimpering thing, cowering away from danger. She jumped in and fought as hard as she could. I'd do well to remember that.

"You helped me when it mattered most," she said. She wiped her eyes and climbed off my lap. When she held out her hand to tug me off the ground, I tried not to laugh as I was so much larger than her.

But I let her help. My mate had proven she was strong today. She did not need to prove anything more.

Fluffy sprang up, her tongue lolling.

"My mother says Fluffy will have pups," I said, waving to the droog.

"She's pregnant?" Awe filled Alexa's voice. "I wonder if anyone wants a puppy?" Her fingers coiled through Fluffy's ruff. "Not that I'll give your babies away fast, sweetie pie. Maybe when they reach a certain age?" She tipped her head back to look up at me. "How many puppies do droogs have in one litter?"

"Eight. Ten." I groaned, realizing how crowded my domit would soon be.

I wouldn't have it any other way. Alexa brought joy to my life.

As we started back across the plain, returning to the village, she released a laugh that still contained a tinge of fear. It hurt my heart to hear that sound coming from my mate's mouth.

Once I was sure she was safe, I'd find Trudar. He'd pay for selling my mate to a dusklen. After that, I would ensure there were no more duskhorde in the area.

Our way of life was changing, in some ways for the better—our Earthling mates—and in others that would soon cause great disarray among the Clans.

We needed to keep the duskhorde away from us permanently, and I might have a plan. I'd discuss it with the elders and warlords, but that was for the next sunslice. Today was for comforting my mate.

I lifted her off her feet and carried her.

"I can walk, you know," she said with a smile.

"I want you in my arms."

Her fingers trailed across the back of my neck and linked together. "It's okay. This is where I want to be, Bruge. With you. Always."

Fourteen Sunslices Later
ALEXA

I slid the last of the bread out of the oven and carefully carried it over to one of the tables. Fifty loaves took a long time to create, knead, and bake. But today I would introduce the Ferlaern to bread.

"It smells amazing," Bruge said, coming up behind me. His arms went around me, and he leaned over to kiss my cheek.

"I sampled it earlier. It tastes amazing, too." Turning in his arms, I kissed him, wishing we could sneak away for some alone time. He lifted me up and—

"Have some bread, Mommy?" Will asked, tugging on the back of my dress.

"Have?" Ben echoed. He hugged Bruge's leg.

I slid down Bruge's front. Interruptions were just another part of our life together.

"Later," I whispered in promise.

His grin widened. So far, no one had interrupted us once we shut the door flap to our bedroom at night.

Give it time.

Bruge strode around me and peeked underneath one of the blankets covering the baskets of sliced bread.

While I'd spent the morning baking the bread we prepared yesterday and let rise overnight, he'd taken the boys to the trundier pen to begin teaching them how to interact with some of the younger beasts.

I bit my tongue a lot lately, struggling not to cling to my boys, but it was getting easier all the time. Bruge loved them as much as me; he'd never let them come to harm.

And they were thriving here, so much more than they had back on Earth.

They were becoming full Ferlaern.

Things had been unsettled since Saldarn and Trudar kidnapped and sold me to the dusklen in exchange for alcohol. Bruge took a fleet of warriors mounted on trundier, and they searched the area but found no evidence of more duskhorde.

No evidence of Trudar either, unfortunately. He was out there somewhere, hopefully running as far away from this area as possible.

"Did you have fun with the trundiers?" I asked the boys.

"I rode," Will said, spreading his arms out by his head. "Wit Bruge."

"Big trundies," Ben said, his eyes wide. "Ride trundies."

"Sounds like an amazing morning."

Fluffy galloped over and nudged Ben's back, making him giggle. He whirled around and clung to the droog's ruff. She waddled; her belly distended like she'd swallowed more than a few basketballs. I couldn't wait until she gave birth to her pups. Piper and Rayne had already put in requests to adopt one, but I wanted to wait until they were born before making decisions about giving them away.

"I was about to ring the bell," I told Ben and Will. "Why don't you boys do it for me?"

Since this was the first time I'd serve bread, we were making it a separate occasion outside our normal mealtime. If things went well, I'd kick up production with the help of warriors interested in learning the baking craft.

Everyone would come here for a sample the moment I announced things were ready.

"I ring," Ben said, his little legs churning as he ran toward the table holding the bell.

"Me, too," Will cried, rushing after him.

I looked over the tables, trying to see if I was missing anything. I'd covered the loaves with blankets to keep the bugs away, and I'd spent the morning slicing in addition to baking with the help of two warriors.

I'd even set out covered crocks of butter, having talked the narlesk milkers into relinquishing some of their cream. Salt came from the mountains; I'd tasted it when we lived in our treetop domits. It wasn't easy churning butter, but there was just enough to go around. Each person could spread a very fine layer on their slice.

"Ring it, younglings," Bruge said, flashing his tusks at me.

The boys lifted the big bell together and shook it; the hollow gong resounded, vibrating within my bones.

Hundreds of Ferlaern left the village and strode up the hill, many with skepticism on their segmented faces.

Like a pied piper, Irella led them up the final incline and over to me.

"Where are the results of all our warrior's hard work?" she asked with a sniff.

Sadly, not much had changed between us. We shared an uneasy truce, mostly maintained to keep Bruge happy.

Would she mock or congratulate me today? It was anyone's guess.

"Allow me to show you." I lifted my voice as I walked to the table. "Everyone! Form a line."

A few grumbled but curiosity won them over. Once they'd quieted in anticipation and stood waiting, I tugged a blanket off one of the tables.

"We will eat…this fluffy light brown mounds?" Irella asked, though thankfully not unkindly. She inched closer to the table.

"You first," I said, striding over to her. I took a slice of still-warm bread, went generous with the butter even though that meant I'd get none, and handed it to her.

"I do not know about this," she said, shooting Bruge a concerned look.

"Eat it," Will said with a laugh.

"Eat," Ben echoed in a softer tone. His eyes gleamed as he stared up at Irella, and when I saw him holding her hand, I realized he liked her. He felt comfortable with her. When had that happened? Sure, she'd been over to our domit a few evenings, asking to play with the boys while we went for a walk or disappeared on Nykas for an hour or so, but she always seemed so stilted with them.

They stood at her sides, watching as she lifted the slice to her mouth.

Most of the crowd watched as well, though a few stepped forward to take their own slices.

Her tusks bit into the bread, and she chewed thoughtfully. Wonder spread across her face, and she gave me a startled look. "It tastes…"

I swore half the group leaned forward, awaiting her words.

"It is delicious." She took another bite then giggled. Actually giggled.

But her laughter faded when her gaze met mine. I read sorrow there and wondered what I did to offend her this time.

I leaned back against Bruge, needing the comfort of his arms. If she hated my offering—still hated me—how would I ever hope to win her?

A sob jerked out of her, and she spun, presenting me with her back. Her body tightened, poised to run, but she only took a few steps before coming to a halt. Her shoulders curled forward.

Ben and Will watched her, as did I.

I looked up at Bruge, wondering if we should do something, but he kept his attention directed at his mother.

She turned and strode back over us.

While I gaped, she dropped to her knees and took my hands.

'I am sorry," she said softly, then louder. "I am sorry! I…" There is no excuse for my behavior except I clung to the old ways rather than accepting that the Ferlaern needed to change if we hoped to survive. I need to change as well." She looked up at me. "Can you forgive me?"

I tugged her up and hugged her while Will and Ben crowded close, clinging to both her dress and mine.

"There's nothing to forgive," I said, my heart overjoyed. "We're family."

Would you like to read a
bonus epilogue from
Seduced by an Alien Warlord?
Sign up for my newsletter,
and it's yours, free.
I think it's time for

alien puppies…

Sign me up!

If you'd like to read Chapter 1 of *Tempted by an Alien Warlord,*
Book 4 in the Fated Mates of the Ferlaern Warriors Series,
turn the page!

If you enjoyed **Bruge & Alexa's** story,
would you leave a review?
It would mean so much to me!
You can leave your review on Amazon.

About the Author

Ava Ross fell for men with unusual features when she first watched Star Wars, where alien creatures have gone mainstream. She lives in New England with her husband (who is sadly not an alien, though he is still cute in his own way), her kids, and a few assorted pets.

Books by Ava

MAIL-ORDER BRIDES OF CRAKAIR

Vork

Bryk

Jorg

Kral

Wulf

Lyel

Axil, Gaje

(companion novellas in one book)

BRIDES OF DRIEGON

Malac

Drace

Rashe

Teran

Kruze, Allor

(companion novellas in one book)

IN LOVE WITH AN ALIEN ANTHOLOGY

Neere

a Brides of Driegon short story

ALIEN EMBRACE ANTHOLOGY

Skoar

a Brides of Driegon novella

FATED MATES OF THE FERLAERN WARRIORS

Enticed by an Alien Warlord

Tamed by an Alien Warlord

Seduced by an Alien Warlord

Tempted by an Alien Warlord

You can find all my books on Amazon.

<hr>

Tempted by an Alien Warlord

<hr>

She hates him (not really).
He hates her (not really?).
But when she's kidnapped by the
duskhorde, he mounts a bold rescue,
only to be captured himself.
Can they escape and find true love together?

Zetar: After losing my mate to the disease, I promised never to love another. Then I meet Josie. She's full of fire, and she tests my patience. I can't decide if I want to storm away from her or kiss her—something that's completely forbidden. But when she's kidnapped by the vicious duskhorde, I go after her. I'll stop at nothing to bring her back to her daughter, though I don't dare bring her back for myself.

Josie: When my thirteen-year-old daughter and I move to Ferlaern, I hope to find love. I don't expect to fall for a guy eleven years younger than me. I'm a thirty-eight-year-old woman, for heaven's sakes, not a blushing teenage.

But *Zetar* sure makes my face—and other parts of me—hot. And despite the fact that he irks the H-E-double-hockey-sticks out of me, he also makes me dream of lounging in bed with him on a Sunday morning. Then I'm kidnapped by the duskhorde. If I don't get free, Zetar and I will never find our happy ending.

Tempted by an Alien Warlord is Book 4 in the Fated Mates of the Ferlaern Warriors Series. This standalone, full-length romance has on-the-page heat, aliens who look and act alien, a guaranteed happily ever after, no cheating, and no cliffhanger. Look for the complete series on Amazon.

Chapter 1
JOSIE

"Zetar, Zetar, Zetar," I growled to my thirteen-going-on-thirty-year-old daughter, Savvy. "I don't want to hear anything else about Zetar."

Sitting on the sofa, Savvy clunked her heels up on the edge of the coffee table. "But—"

"Please. No." I held up my hand, though I gave her a kind look. She meant well. As for Zetar…

Damn hot alien horde dude. A month ago, he kissed up to me and then he kissed me.

Talk about sending my mind into outer space. I'd kissed lots of guys in my thirty-eight-years. His wasn't any different than them. Well, all right. I will admit it if only to me. His kiss was amazing. Like, I essentially saw fireworks and felt all that heat flaring in my groin stuff I've read about in romance novels.

When he lifted me off my feet and pressed me against the tree, his big, erect cock ground against me where I wanted him most.

This is it, I thought. We were heading into hop-into-bed territory.

Despite him being younger than me, things were going to work out. Our age difference didn't matter to him. Neither did my gray hairs—fairy strands, Savvy called them.

But when I moaned and wrapped my legs around him, riding that glorious cock through his pants, his head jerked up. His eyes filled with sorrow then steely resolve.

He unlinked my arms from around his neck, my legs from around his waist, and mumbled something about needing to go take care of an injured narlesk.

When I sought him out the next morning, he told me he didn't have time for a relationship with an Earthling.

"You're worried about rejection," Savvy said. She rose and rounded the sofa, stopping in front of me where I stood near the door.

Where I stood wishing I could escape through the door.

She stroked my face like she was the mom and me the teenager. "After your experience growing up, I understand why you worry about rejection."

"This has nothing to do with that," I said, stepping backward.

Hell, if anyone understood what Zetar meant when he said he wasn't interested in more, it was me. I grew up in foster care and for me, that meant complete rejection.

"I know some of the homes you lived in had kind parents and some did not," Savvy said, unwilling to let this go, for some reason.

"I've told you this before. The cute, younger kids got adopted. The cute, older kids got new clothes and went to college. Skinny, gangly me did none of the above."

"You were kicked out of the last "home" the moment you turned eighteen, which is a total fuckathon."

"Language."

She smirked, but she wouldn't take it back. She got her sailor mouth from me.

"Zetar is not your foster parents," she said.

He wasn't, but he didn't want me any more than they did. If that was how he felt, I no longer wanted him.

"Things are different here," Savvy said. "If only you'd talk with him. Hell, I've talked with him. He's—"

"He's not creeping on you, is he?" I half-shouted. If he thought he'd—

"Yuck, no!" She rolled her eyes. "Jeez, Mom. Do you really think he'd… Well, I guess you do or you wouldn't say it. He's helped me with Bindy. That's all."

Savvy loved that young trundier she was bonding with like it was a full sibling.

"I wasn't sure if I wanted anything to do with him at first," she said, her head tilting. Sunlight slanted through the room, gliding across her beautiful brown face so like my own. "Zetar's okay. Give him time, and he grows on you."

"If he does anything you don't feel comfortable with, you come to me right away," I said.

"Mom!" She dropped her voice and rolled her eyes again. "It's nothing like that. Crap. He acts more like a dad than anything else. Get the creepster idea out of your mind this second." Her mouth quirked up on one side, and she took my hand, pleading. "Trust me. He's a nice guy. I think he likes you. Give him a chance, and you'd see."

"It's not… We're not compatible." A lame excuse but the only one I could come up with on the fly.

I hadn't told her about his rejection, and I sure didn't intend to tell her now. My daughter and I shared a lot of things, but my heartache wasn't one of them. It was too much of a burden to place on a teen.

"If he was interested in me, he'd show it," I said with finality. "And he hasn't."

"He won your basket at the secret auction."

"He bid on it by mistake."

"I told him it was yours before the auction started."

Jeez! I stomped my foot, a totally little kid move. "That was supposed to remain secret," I groused. "It was part of the rules."

She shrugged. "I wanted him to know it was yours."

Hell, had he bid on it out of pity?

I was older than the other Earth women. Sure, Ferlaern guys were friendly to me; there were practically no females here, so almost any woman would do. It didn't mean they were interested in me for who I was inside.

I growled as I paced in front of her. "Why is this so important to you?"

"Because I can tell you're not happy."

That comment brought my steps to a halt. Unwelcome tears sprang up in my eyes, and I blinked fast to dispel them. "I'm happy. What gives you the idea I'm not?"

"I know you, Mom," she said softly. "It's been just you and me all my life."

"We had Steve, your wonderful father."

"He was amazing." Her voice broke. "I miss Dad all the time. He was the best dad in the world, and no one will ever replace him." Her chin lifted. "But he wasn't your lover."

I snorted. "It sure wasn't immaculate conception."

"You used artificial insemination."

I swallowed my surprise and it didn't go down easy. Pausing by the sofa, I traced my finger along the back. "What gave you that idea?"

"Dad told me. He was gay." She chuckled. "I would've figured it out even if he hadn't told me. He liked guys and that was awesome. But he didn't love you other than as a sister."

"We were best friends."

"Which made you amazing parents. Frankly, you should've had more kids together."

We'd tried but something was damaged after Savvy and I was told the odds of having more were slim.

Savvy stiffened her spine. "Here's the thing. Your heart is so big, it could swallow the world. You deserve a love of a lifetime."

This girl of mine amazed me all the time. How could I respond to something like that? Turning, I leaned against the sofa. "And you think that's Zetar?"

"I think it could be."

"Why?"

"Because he watches you with his heart in his eyes."

My breath caught, but I shoved it out with my surprise. "We took a few walks together, talked, but that was it." And shared a wonderful kiss and grinding session—more details not to mention to my daughter. "He doesn't love me."

"Maybe and maybe not, but I think he could." She stepped closer, keeping her pace easy, as if she thought I'd flee. Frankly, I wanted to, but she was between me and the door. "Something happened between you two. You went from happy to sad, and at first, I thought it was because you didn't like it here on Ferlaern. Then I saw the same look in his eyes, and I guessed. You don't need to tell me what happened between you two. That's for you and Zetar to discuss. But maybe you should pin him down and listen if he wants to talk?"

"You're too wise for your own good." I said it with complete kindness. If my heart could swallow the world, Savvy's could take on the entire galaxy. My daughter gave life everything she had and found a way to keep giving after that.

"Just tell me you'll try. If the opportunity comes up, give him a chance. He's mentioned things to me… If he pushed you away, I think he has reasons."

"Mentioned what?" Leave it me to hone in that part of her statement.

A full smile bloomed on her face, and it hit me in the gut. She looked so much like Steve, it hurt. I missed my friend more than anything.

"Ask him, and I bet he'll tell you," she said.

I stiffened. "All right, I will." Someday. Not today when my insides still felt raw. "I've got to go check on the wounded trundier." The animal healers were doing all they could for it, but they'd asked me to take a look. As a nurse back on Earth, I wasn't used to treating patients that looked like giant hornets, but empathy was a common thing in my profession. We sensed what our patients were feeling, and would do what we could to help them get better.

"I'll see you at the dining domit later, then?" she said. "I'll go see if Alexa would like me to take the boys for a walk. I'm sure she and Bruge would like a second or two to think."

My daughter inherited my empathy. She could sense when others had need and she went out of her way to deliver.

"That's nice of you. And sure, let's meet up for dinner. At sunset?" We had no clocks here and basically gauged time by the sun's location in the sky.

She nodded.

Grabbing the medical bag I brought from Earth, I nudged aside the door flap and stepped out onto the path. I ran right into someone hurrying past my domit.

His hands braced my forearms, and I stared up at him, squirming inside.

"Zetar," I said. Naturally I'd run into him and no one else.

"I'm glad we've met up," he said in that deep, gravelly voice that made my pheromones perk up and zing through me. "I wish to speak with you, Josie, if you have a munette."

Despite implying I'd listen to Zetar, when the moment was at hand, I bolted.

"Not time," I said, tugging away and scampering down the path away from him.

I kept going, not stopping when he called my name, his voice full of exasperation.

When I reached the fence partitioning the trundiers from the village, I stopped and looked back.

Zetar had not followed me.

See? He didn't want to talk to me that badly.

Hours later, after I'd given the trundier a dose of medicine I'd concocted under Elder Narcial's guidance, I repacked my medical bag and shouldered it. I shoved stray hairs off my face and looked down at my grubby clothes. A few slaps of my hand did nothing to eliminate the grime ground in from crawling beneath the creature to sneak up on its snout. It wasn't easy shoving tincture down a giant hornet's throat.

Lights from the village spilled in this direction, but shadows dominated this area.

It seemed I was alone, other than the trundiers.

A few Ferlaern warriors had gathered to watch while I cared for the beast I diagnosed as having eaten something it shouldn't have. A glance toward the fence told me they'd left.

So had the sun.

Shit. Savvy asked to meet at the dining domit at sunset, and I was late!

I hurried toward the fence and ducked between the rails. When I straightened, a subtle sound behind me made me turn. I squinted but couldn't determine what it could be. It hadn't come from the pen but from beyond...

Only a vast plain of wavering grass watched me, plus a few trees that created shadows where someone could hide.

My spine quivered, and my mouth went dry.

"I'm not afraid," I whispered. "There's nothing out there but a few random narlesks, and they're mostly friendly."

Also vicious zithers, but they didn't come close to the village—too many warriors around.

My skin prickling, I turned back and started up the path. The sooner I returned to the others, the sooner I'd be safe.

Footsteps rushed up behind me.

I twisted, my medical bag slipping from my shoulder. As it thumped on the ground, someone grabbed my hair. He hauled me close, and his big arm snapped around my neck, pinning my back to his chest.

"Don't make a sound," he hissed.

Was this Trudar? I couldn't tell, but it must be. Horror burst through me. Trudar kidnapped Alexa and sold her to the duskhorde. After the Ferlaern rescued her, they searched but didn't find him.

I flailed, kicking and smacking him, but an Earthling

female was no match for a Ferlaern warrior almost twice her size.

He hauled me backward, my heels catching in the dirt as he dragged me.

When I shrieked, he clamped his grubby hand over my mouth.

His hot breath singed my ear. "I told you, no sound." The male released my mouth only long enough to press a scrap of material over my face. It smelled like…a sour herb.

The village lights flickered. My mind swam through mud.

Savvy… My little girl.

No…

If you'd like to read more, you can find
Tempted by an Alien Warlord here.